Adventures of a Country Preacher:

Fiery Trials, Weary Miles, and Happy Smiles

Adventures of a Country Preacher:

Fiery Trials, Weary Miles, and Happy Smiles

Angel Enfinger Crain

ISBN: 978-1-6964-1700-6 *(paperback)*

ASIN: B07ZXJZ775 *(eBook)*

LCCN: 2019918595

First paperback edition December 2019

Printed in the United States of America

A special thanks to the talented Karin King Harms for her time and attention to the editorial aspects of this book.

To my Dad, my role model, and my hero.

I will forever be your number one fan and will always remain your little girl. Thank you for inspiring the stories reflected within these pages and for always showing me what it means to truly have a servant's heart. I have seen you give your all to those who lacked appreciation and gratitude, I have witnessed your struggles, both physically and emotionally, I have watched you with admiration through some of the toughest trials and some of the most desperate of circumstances. Through every fiery trial, you pressed on. Over many a weary mile, you endured. Even on your darkest days, your humor has always afforded you the ability to smile.

Table of Contents

Chapter 1 - Spring 1980 2

Chapter 2 - Trials and Faith 14

Chapter 3 - Bolting Buck 26

Chapter 4 - Valley View 1982 34

Chapter 5 - Allelujahs and Amens 38

Chapter 6 - India 45

Chapter 7 - Coastal Complications 58

Chapter 8 - Picking up the Pieces 71

Chapter 9 - Baldwin Beginnings 82

Chapter 10 - Rooted 'til Retirement 87

Chapter 11 - Branching Out 95

Chapter 12 - Recovering and Rejoicing 107

Chapter 13 - Tragedy and Loss 115

Chapter 14 - Excitement and Emergency 123

Chapter 15 - Dealing with Difficulty 132

Chapter 16 - Second Arrest 139

Chapter 17 - Care-giving Clergy 147

Chapter 18 - Managing Medical Mysteries and Ministry 161

Chapter 19 - Making Sense of It All 168

Epilogue 177

Chapter 1

As the old preacher recollected the events of Spring 1980, he could not help but to shudder. Reverend Warren Englewilde had been so young, so inexperienced in everything. He had surrendered to preach when he was only fifteen years old. He had been preaching all over the Florida Panhandle and beyond since before he even had a driver's license. Briefly, he had pastored Country Road Baptist Church just over the Alabama/Florida state line in the little community of Rosinton. He had been only 18 when they called him and it had proved to be a challenge for such a young man to pastor some very set-in-their-ways adults. The two years he stayed there as pastor had seemed to last an eternity. He had pastored while attending classes at Mobile College after marrying just before the dawn of the 80s. It had all been a lot for him to juggle but failure was not an option. At only 21 years of age, he found himself pastoring his second church, Bethlehem Baptist Church in Flomaton, Alabama. He may not have been much older when Bethlehem called him, but he felt a little wiser after dealing with some of the small-town squabbles he had faced at Rosinton.

Being newly married and having preached for nearly six years at the time, he felt anxious to begin a great and mighty work for the Lord during this pastorate. He had approached his congregation with the idea to purchase a van to be used to transport children and families to church; people who would otherwise have no means of transportation to attend services. One family in particular was from the nearby Poarch Creek Indian reservation and had very little education. They were very poor and Rev. Englewilde's heart ached for the two small children in the home. Fred and his wife, Gladys, were eager to ride the van with their children and attend services. However, being uneducated and steeped in the traditions of their Poarch Creek heritage, they were somewhat under the thumb of Gladys' father Floyd.

Floyd was illiterate and did not wish for anyone to tamper with his family. He enjoyed ruling them with an iron fist and strongly disliked the preacher and the church's attempts to offer aid to his daughter and her family. He and his wife lived at the top of Hudson Hill in Century, Florida. Fred and Gladys resided at the bottom, under the watchful eye of Floyd. No one came to visit Fred and Gladys without Floyd being fully aware of the visit and all that transpired.

While they lived in Florida across the state line from Bethlehem Baptist Church in Alabama, the distance was only a matter of a couple miles.

Regardless of Floyd's disapproval, the church began to transport the small family to services. Fred, Gladys, and their 6-year-old son all trusted the Lord as their Savior within a few months. Floyd did not like the idea of his family venturing off to do their own thing apart from the entire family unit. Floyd could not control the aspect of their lives that included the church and Rev. Englewilde because he was not a part of it; this greatly upset him. While he attended church services on a few occasions, he only showed interest in order to receive gifts from the church. On one occasion, the church flooded the homes of both Floyd and Fred with clothes, food, and other necessities. The following week, Floyd hosted a yard sale and sold all that the church people had gifted to his poverty-stricken family. The majority of Bethlehem Baptist Church was elderly and on fixed incomes. It greatly affected the parishioners to see the way their gifts to this family were sold off just a couple of miles from the church's steeple. Many did not wish to further assist this family, for fear any future gifts would be handled in the same manner.

Regardless of ole Floyd's feelings on the issue, Fred and Gladys continued to ride the church van to services with their children. After a while, Gladys became pregnant. The ladies of the church showered her with baby gifts and did what they could to help her prepare for the arrival of their new baby. One morning Fred called Rev. Englewilde to tell him that Gladys was in the hospital, suffering excruciating abdominal pain. Within a few days, she gave birth to a stillborn baby. It was revealed that the child had died several days prior in the womb, but the hospital was overcrowded and Gladys lacked insurance. She had been in pain and the hospital had failed to realize that the baby inside her had died. She lay there in pain until her body finally went into labor and she gave birth all alone in the hospital room. Her screams of shock, horror, and grief alerted the hospital staff to the issue and they rushed to her side, too little, too late. Rev. Englewilde arranged for Gladys to be taken home to rest after this unexpected and tragic loss. She requested that Pastor Englewilde inform her father that she was home. Arrangements were made for a small graveside service and Gladys asked the preacher to plan to say a few words before they buried her infant. The preacher slowly along the dusty drive that led between Gladys' house and her father's. The entire family lived in a cluster of run-down shotgun houses on a hill. None of them held down steady jobs and they always seemed to be lurking around the yard or porch. He felt surrounded and closed in as he rolled to a stop.

When Pastor Englewilde arrived at Floyd's house, he was not met with any modicum of friendliness. Floyd answered the door and grabbed the young preacher by the tie, dragging him inside and forcefully shoving him onto the couch. One of Floyd's grown daughters, Ginger, who outweighed the poor young preacher by about 150 pounds, leaned her large frame against the door, blocking his nearest exit. A flood of fear washed over Rev. Englewilde as Floyd dispatched some of his other children throughout the house and began to berate the preacher with a barrage of expletives. In the course of his ranting and raving, Floyd grabbed a machete from a hook on the wall. He began to wave it around and threaten the preacher if he ever attempted to step foot in Fred and Gladys' home again. In a half-drunken rage, he waved the machete in the preacher's face, exclaiming, "I can take care of my daughter! We don't need you or your help. If you step foot on our property again, I will kill you, Preacher!" The wiry preacher began to pray, not openly but inwardly, that the Lord would guide him and control the situation. He was resolved that if Floyd did not calm down, he would have no choice but to barrel through the nearest plate glass window and desperately race to his car before the man with the machete could catch him. Rev. Englewilde remembers the specific words he prayed, "Lord, I am fixin' to go through that window if this man doesn't calm down. I can't go through the door because of this woman and I can't go through the door down the hallway because Floyd has sent his son and wife back there and, for all I know, the boy has a gun pointed on me back there. So, Lord, either calm the situation down, or I'm going through that window!" All this was prayed internally as he kept his eyes trained on the raving man with a machete in front of him and the giant woman still barricading the closest door.

As the preacher completed his internal prayer, Floyd seemed to calm down. He walked over and hung the machete back on its hook and said, "Preacher, I'm going to let you go, but if you come back to my daughter's house or my house, I will see to it that you die. And I've got enough family, we can do that." Ginger moved away from the door. Rev. Englewilde carefully rose from the couch and walked over to the door. As he reached out and took the doorknob in his hand his bravery and courage began to blossom. With each step, his chances of escaping this crazy scenario still breathing were improving by leaps and bounds. The fear in his throat, fueled by adrenaline, turned to stubborn defiance. The pounding in his ears and the fresh air streaming in from the cracked doorway empowered him, as if the Holy Spirit had breathed down sweet reassurance from Heaven. He opened the door a couple inches, feeling a bit bolder by the second. As he gripped the doorknob firmly and took his first step into the freedom the broken down old front porch offered, he turned to look at Floyd and said, "Floyd, let me tell you something. The funeral is tomorrow at 2 o'clock and your daughter has asked me to do the funeral and I will be at that graveside tomorrow at 2 o'clock." Floyd's rage began to flare up again as he spewed back at the preacher, "No you won't be there. I have a friend who will handle the service. You will not be allowed to attend." Feeling emblazoned with courage, the preacher replied, "You do what you have to do, Floyd, but I will be there." With that, he ran to the car and fought to keep himself from vomiting, he was so overcome by fear, panic, relief, and justified anger. By the time he arrived at his home, his boldness had grown exponentially, having removed himself from immediate physical threat of harm. He immediately called his preacher friend, Rev. Townsend and recounted to him all of the events of the day. Rev. Townsend pastored in the neighboring town across the Florida state line. He was slightly older and had always been a mentor and friend to the young preacher. They regularly enjoyed meeting to fellowship, pray, and compare sermon notes. Upon hearing of Rev. Englewilde's intent to attend the funeral against Floyd's wishes, Rev. Townsend offered to accompany him to visit Fred and Gladys, then to join him at the funeral service as well. Rev. Townsend had attended school with Gladys and felt safe visiting her. He advised Rev. Englewilde to report what had transpired with the local police, just as a precaution should Floyd attempt to harm him.

At the police station, Rev. Englewilde was asked if he would like to press charges. He considered that the incident had transpired in Floyd's home and that it would be impossible to prove what had happened. He knew the members of that household would corroborate any story Floyd decided to tell in his own defense. The police agreed that no charges could be filed, but a report was made to keep a record of the altercation should anything actually happen to the pastor or his young bride. A copy of this report was kept on file and the police offered to have a squad car in place at the time of the graveside funeral to deter any notions of ill will toward the preacher.

The next morning, Rev. Englewilde and his wife were out making visits to shut-in parishioners and he drove her past the cemetery where he was to perform the funeral later that day. As he slowed to point it out to her, he saw people gathered around the grave which was to be the resting place for Fred and Gladys' child. He later found out that Floyd had changed the time of the funeral service and had told his grieving daughter that the preacher had refused to come, leading the bereaved Gladys and Fred to be deeply hurt by their preacher's absence. Rev. Englewilde immediately went to get Rev. Townsend and they went to pay a visit to Gladys and Frank to apologize for not knowing the time of the service had been secretly changed. They found a very brokenhearted Gladys upon their arrival.

She was distraught at the loss of her baby and hurt that her minister had not been there as he had promised. After speaking, Gladys and Rev. Englewilde then realized the full extent of Floyd's deceit.

That evening during the midweek worship service, Rev. Englewilde shared with his congregation what had transpired with Gladys, her baby, and the funeral services earlier that day. Moved with compassion, the people of the congregation scrambled around to collect groceries and casseroles to be taken as a way of encouragement to the grieving family. Dan, a deacon in the church, offered to go with the preacher to deliver the goods. On their way back through town, Dan asked the preacher to stop by his office for a brief moment. Rev. Englewilde sat in the car and waited a few minutes then they were on their way back to the church where the preacher went back to his study to prepare Sunday's sermon.

About two weeks later, Floyd got abducted by the Ku Klux Klan. Three men wearing white hoods and bed sheets came to where Floyd was doing some odd jobs and yard work for a prominent man in the community. They drove up, hit him several times, and then stuffed him in the back floorboard of their car and sped away. They took him into the woods and commenced to beating him with a leather strap. While beating him, they gave him a lecture in which they listed five reasons why he deserved what he was getting: 1) Dealing drugs 2)

Making moonshine 3) Incest with his daughters 4) Beating his wife 5) Threatening to kill the preacher. Needless to say, reason #5 implicated Rev. Englewilde. The three men beat Floyd pretty good and turned him loose. He was found wandering down a dirt road in the dark and taken to County Hospital, where they treated him and sent him home that night. The attackers had used a stick or club in addition to the leather strap, so little DNA evidence would have been found to incriminate the attackers, had police known to look for such things in the 1980s.

Naturally, the hospital notified the police at the first mention of a KKK attack in the 1980s and, when questioned, Floyd told investigators emphatically that the preacher had done it, having remembered the mention of him in the midst of his attack. The police furthered questioned Floyd, asking him how he could be sure if all faces had been covered. Floyd replied, "I recognized his voice from up under the hood."

Now, for some this may seem implausible but in Rev. Englewilde's case, his voice is extremely identifiable and unique. It has been reasoned that this unique voice is due to the fact that he began preaching at a young age, an age in which most boys develop their voices as they begin to change with puberty. It is speculated by some that the manner in which he has always preached could have perhaps stripped out some gears in the vocal box, so to speak. Those who have heard on tape his early sermons from his teen years have noted that the high pitch in which he spoke, combined with the extremely fast pace of his speech sounded something akin to Mickey Mouse on steroids. And for those who may find this overly critical and harsh in regards to his voice, it is important to note that Rev. Englewilde himself came up with this succinct analogy to describe how these recordings sounded to him personally.

So, with Floyd's testimony that he heard the preacher's unmistakable voice on that fateful evening in the woods, the illiterate old man dictated what he said had happened and placed his X on the bottom of the paper, acknowledging that the preacher had beat him up. Based upon his sworn statement, an investigation was launched against Rev. Englewilde in search of a connection between him and the KKK. The police posted a watch across the street from the church and kept a log of each vehicle that came and went. They watched the parishioners as well as the pastor, in hopes of finding that connection. Within a couple of weeks, the chief of police phoned Rev. Englewilde and asked him to come to the station to be arrested.

Without knowing the details of the beating or having any intimate knowledge of any KKK members, Rev. Englewilde was arrested on the charges of attempted murder and kidnapping on March 11, 1981.

Chapter 2

While Rev. Englewilde had the support of family and friends, the charges were a gut punch to the preacher. The investigators politely explained to him that Deacon Dan had set the whole thing up. They believed that Dan had made a phone call on that quick stop at the office while driving with the preacher from Fred and Gladys' home and that the phone call had started the chain of events leading to Floyd's beating. At the time of that call, Dan was already under investigation for his involvement with the Klan. He had inadvertently set the preacher up while he was inside his office on the phone explaining to his fellow clansman why Floyd deserved punishment. Dan made sure people knew that he was with the preacher so he could use him as his own alibi, should he need one. Dan was arrested, as well as the man who had employed Floyd in the odd jobs. That man was a prominent, middle-aged businessman by the name of Rich who had aspirations to hold public office. The idea that he had hired a man twice his age to do yard work seemed suspicious to the police and they felt that the coincidence of Floyd's presence on his property in conjunction with the connection he had with Dan were just cause to bring Rich in. Law enforcement considered their luring of Floyd to the job to be a form of kidnapping, especially since he was found wandering alone after dark, beaten and disoriented. Because Floyd's abduction and beating by the KKK took place by crossing the Florida/ Alabama state line several times by several of the guilty parties, the FBI was brought in to work on the case, alongside the Alabama Bureau of Investigations and local law enforcement from both Century, Florida and Flomaton, Alabama.

To say that the young Rev. Englewilde was scared would be a severe understatement. He had never laid eyes on Rich to his recollection and he was completely unaware of Deacon Dan's involvement with either the Klan or the crime against Floyd. But proving his innocence seemed an insurmountable task to the young preacher.

He immediately called Rev. Townsend to meet him at the county jail to post bail. It was to their advantage that Rev. Townsend knew the judge and small-town politics were very much in play. As Rev. Townsend entered the county jail, Rev. Englewilde was in the process of being fingerprinted and booked in the next room. The fiery Rev. Townsend approached the rookie cop behind the desk and demanded, "Where's Warren?!" Rev. Townsend was not one with which to trifle. His no-nonsense manner had a way of putting others on notice not to toy with him. He was serious and his presence and demeanor demanded respect. His beady eyes bore into the soul of the officer as the officer replied, "We don't have anyone here by that name." Rev. Townsend had little patience and expressed as much when he retorted, "I know he is here, too, and I demand to see Warren Englewilde!" Rev. Englewilde popped his head out of the adjoining door and calmed his friend, saying, "Hey, man, I'm right here; just calm down. There's no need for both of us to wind up in here. I'm ok. Somebody has got to stay on the outside."

The preacher had a gift for using humor to diffuse the toughest of situations. It was one of his strengths, although some may argue it was a weakness at times. He inherited this ability from his mother. She could find the humor in things, as well. Laughter was their medicine in times of adversity.

The little rookie officer stood shocked at the scene that had unfolded upon Rev. Townsend's entrance and replied that he had thought the person in question may have been an employee rather than an inmate. Rev. Townsend was allowed to stay with Rev. Englewilde while he awaited a bond hearing before the judge; more of that "small town politics" mentality at work.

Neither of the men had any money on them and neither of them owned their own land in the state because they each resided in homes provided for them by the churches they pastored. According to state law at the time, one must own land in order to post bond. Exceptions were made because of Rev. Townsend's reputation in the area as a local minister. This was one of the few instances that small town politics has worked to the little man's advantage. In this case, bond was posted and Rev. Englewilde was sent home, not having to withstand a night in jail.

On the drive home, Rev. Englewilde filled his friend in on what the sheriff deputy had told him on his transport drive to the county jail. The officer had looked at him and said, "Look, preacher, we know you aren't guilty but we know you know people that are. I don't know if you know what they did or who they are, but Dan is guilty as a snake in Hell. You may not know that but we know that if we put enough pressure on you, we will get the guilty culprits. Just don't panic. You're gonna get out of this." The words had been a relief to the young preacher, but the reality of the being fingerprinted and having a mug shot could not be ignored. While he had reflected upon the deputy's words throughout the booking process, he still doubted any escape from the charges. It was surreal. Of course, none of that conversation would be printed in the subsequent newspaper articles highlighting the case against the preacher. The newspaper articles written about the case only fed his fear of the unknown. Here he was, just getting hit footing as a young pastor and still in the newlywed stages of his marriage, and his entire career in the ministry looked to be in jeopardy.

Rev. Englewilde hired a lawyer and the case went to court. The entire process took ten and a half months and aged that young man by a decade, it seemed. So much uncertainty was encircling his life. During the months he was under investigation he had attempted to live life as normally as he possibly could. He and his young bride conceived their first child amid the chaos and expense of paying lawyers and court fees, all the while serving in a church made up of at least a few shady characters.

It turned out that Deacon Dan's entire defense was, "I was with the preacher". On the night in question, Rev. Englewilde was scheduled to preach in a county-wide evangelism conference two hours away. It had been widely publicized and there were many in attendance to verify his whereabouts for that night. Deacon Dan had volunteered to drive the preacher to and from the conference, thus sealing himself an alibi at the preacher's side while his friends in robes abducted and beat poor old Floyd. It came out in investigation that the group deliberately set the preacher up and used his name during the beating because they knew he had a solid alibi with around 300 witnesses and could never be placed at the scene of the crime. This fact also made it impossible for Floyd to be telling the truth when he said he had recognized the preacher's voice. When this was brought to light, the charges against Rev. Englewilde were dropped to a reduced charge of conspiracy to commit murder and kidnapping; this was an effort to cajole a plea deal out of the preacher. Unwilling to confess to a crime he absolutely did not commit, nor was he aware of its planning; he refused to take the plea. People from his past as well as his present began to flood the judge with letters in an attempt to plead his case. He had surrendered to preach at the age of fifteen and was in his early twenties at the time of the trial, so he had years' worth of parishioners and family friends backing him up with letters of support, encouragement, and appeal. This first true test of his faith was proving to be one in which he could see the miraculous and merciful hand of God touching his life in about as real a way as possible.

On the day of the trial, the courtroom was packed with people there on behalf of Rev. Englewilde. His parents were both there, of course, along with his wife and friends from church. But in addition to those were countless others: elementary school teachers, high school teachers, other preachers and ministers. They all came in support of Rev. Englewilde and to show that they stood behind his innocence. In all, there were over 200 people in the courtroom.

The docket had been set and the judge began to call out case numbers to be tried. After the first five names were deemed a no-show due to complications with a transport van from county jail, the judge threw his gavel down in exasperation and said, "If nobody is here for their court date, why the **** is my courtroom so full?" The assistant D.A. informed him, "They're here for the preacher, Your Honor." The judge replied, "Well hell, let's try the preacher!" Rev. Englewilde cut his eyes at his father and remarked, "They're mighty flippant with my life."

The young preacher was escorted to a small room and the witnesses were placed in another room, allowing the jury selection process to begin. Young Rev. Englewilde sat hopelessly in that room facing 20 years in prison. In that moment, he took very little solace in the reassurances of the deputy from all those months before. He took little comfort in the letters which had been written on his behalf. He knew in that moment that his only hope rested in the hands of God. His lawyer tried to comfort him, informing him that he had had coffee with both the district attorney and the judge the night before, and everything was going to be ok. Again, there is an example of some of that small-town politics in play. The preacher wondered if it would truly work out to his benefit after all. His lawyer reassured him once again that all would be ok and left the room. When he returned, he offered another deal in which the charges would once again be reduced, leaving him to face a fine but no serious jail time. Adamant that he would not take a deal to plead guilty to a crime he did not commit, the preacher experienced a new surge of panic. Why were they insistent that he plead guilty? They'd told him not to worry, yet they were giving him more than a few causes for concern. He looked his lawyer square in the eyes and said, "I have told you the truth. You know everything I knew before the fact, which is nothing. The only thing I know of this crime is what these cops and you lawyers have told me. Everything I have told you is true. Am I guilty of what they want me to plead to??" His lawyer replied that he was not. "Then tell them to take their best shot. I will not get on the stand under oath and swear to a lie. And if I'm not guilty, bless God, I'm not going to tell them I'm guilty! They can put me in prison if they want to, but I am not saying I am guilty!" His lawyer exited the room to deliver Rev. Englewilde's message to the district attorney. The jury had been selected. Trial was to commence. After a few minutes, he returned to offer yet one more reduced charge: criminal solicitation. They wanted the preacher to say that he had tried to solicit someone to commit a felony crime. The fine for the plea would be $100 and would be seen as no more serious than a traffic violation on his permanent record. Rev. Englewilde thought for a moment. He looked up at his lawyer, and asked him, "Am I guilty?" The lawyer replied that if everything he had said was true then he was not guilty of criminal solicitation. "Then go back and tell them I am not taking the deal. I ain't lying for nobody. If my mama walked in here right now and told me she was guilty, I would turn my mama in to the police. I'm that honest and that straight. I would put my mama in jail for breaking the law. I am not going to confess to something I did not do!" The lawyer stood there a moment and replied, "Men of principle and courtrooms do not go well together. If this goes to trial, you face serious time in jail. If you take this deal, you pay $100 blessed dollars and go home." The preacher asked if he could have someone come in and talk to him before he answered. He requested that his father be sent in to offer him some counsel. His father and wife came in to speak with him. Rev. Englewilde explained the offer to them. He then had his lawyer explain it to them as well. When the lawyer was done, Rev. Englewilde's wife said, "You may want to consider that. A hundred dollars and it's over with." The young preacher turned to face his father and asked him, "What do you think, Daddy?" At that moment, Rev. Englewilde learned a lesson that has stuck with him for the past several decades. His father looked at him and said, "Son, right now, the only thing you can think about is how to get out from under this pressure. But you should never make a major, life-altering decision when you are under pressure. Right now, you're just thinking about escaping the pressure, but six months from now or six years from now, you may be facing a committee of people who are considering calling you as their pastor and you will have to explain to them why you went into a court of law and admitted you were guilty of committing a crime. That will stick with you for the rest of your life, so make sure you are willing to pay that price." With tears in his eyes and an emblazoned resolve to prove once and for all that he was innocent, Rev. Englewilde instructed his lawyer to let the courtroom know to get ready. He would accept no deal and if they wanted to send a man of God to jail, his innocent blood could be on the conscience of the judge and jury. The lawyer excused himself once again to turn down the latest plea deal. Several minutes passed in which the young preacher replayed in his mind the past few months. This had all been a result of is desire to help poor Fred and Gladys. He had taken a special interest in the poor couple and their small family, unknowingly setting Floyd into a jealous tailspin, which resulted in more hatred and malice. His heart for people had left him vulnerable to the unseen ugliness that lurked in the hearts and minds of a few wolves in his congregation. As he sat on the precipice of his unknown future, facing a trial with no certain outcome, he had to make a decision in that moment to trust God no matter what the world may throw at him. In a circumstance that could have potentially weakened his faith and resolve, Rev. Englewilde remained resilient in the face of adversity. After an excruciating few minutes, which no doubt seemed like an eternity, his lawyer returned.

Once again, the young preacher felt himself slipping into different levels of shock and acceptance when he heard his lawyer utter the words, "You are free to go."

He sat there, unable to process this new information. Just moments ago, he had been informed that the jury was selected and courtroom was prepared for his trial. It was truly an Abraham moment, in which God had tested the extent and strength of his faith. After investigating the preacher, his connections, and many in his congregation, charges against Rev. Englewilde were officially dropped on December 15, 1981. He called their bluff when he refused to take the multiple deals he was offered. The judge then saw full well that he was innocent as he had maintained. Not only were all charges dropped, but the judge ordered that his record be expunged, never to show up again. Deacon Dan took a deal and was happy to do so, considering he was "as guilty as sin" according to the judge. The third man involved was actually in the KKK, was an active participant in the beating, and, because of his deep connections within the KKK, his charges had been dropped the day of the arrest. He had never faced any fear of imprisonment or trial; more of those small-town politics at work. He went on to hold a prominent political position in town a few years later.

At the news of the preacher's release and that the charges had been dismissed, a celebration ensued. Those who had come to support him gathered on the courthouse steps and sang hymns of praise. Announcements were made on the local radio broadcasts. Updated news articles were printed, praising the release of the local preacher. Rev. Englewilde and his wife were able to spend a happy Christmas season together, free from the threat of imprisonment and separation. A burden that the preacher had carried on his shoulders for almost a year had been lifted. He had learned a lot about his own faith and character in the course of those months. While he had made stands in the past in his young life, nothing had tested him in the way this incident had, and he was eternally grateful to emerge from the trial a stronger man, more determined than ever to stand for right in all things.

Chapter 3

In the weeks leading up to the birth of his first child, Rev. Englewilde was destined to go through yet another trial. His faith had been tested throughout the ordeal involving the KKK, during which he suffered emotionally in the roller coaster turn of events involving arrest, serious allegations, and possible imprisonment. With that behind him, he began to slowly relax and enjoy life once again. He was looking forward to the birth of his first child. He and his wife focused on the impending birth and eagerly anticipated becoming parents for the first time.

On February 11, 1982, Rev. Englewilde's brother invited him to go deer hunting with him. The boys had been raised in the woods growing up. Their father, part Creek Indian by birth, was familiar with all the sloughs and creek branches throughout the county they grew up in and had taught them from an early age how to fish and hunt. Hunting down deer and wild hogs was as natural to Rusty as preaching was to Rev. Englewilde. Rusty had entered the railroad business and it was his job to maintain the railroad crossings all throughout Escambia county. Many of those crossings could be found in prime deer hunting country. They had each found their calling in their respective fields very early on. Being raised to excel in the arts of outdoor sportsmanship, they took solace in hunting and fishing; the same kind of solace that some get from reading, or meditating, or yoga. This was their comfort zone. The woods of the northwest Florida panhandle were a second home to them and had provided many hours of brotherly bonding throughout their lifetimes. So, on that fateful day, it seemed like just another run-of-the-mill hunting expedition. Rev. Englewilde and Rusty took off for the woods, in search of a deer or two.

It was in the final days of hunting season and the only weapon legal to use at that point in Florida was the black powder rifle. They went down a dirt road, one they had taken several times before, searching for the perfect place to spot a deer. Within just a short period of time, Rusty had a buck in his sights. He took aim and fired, missing the buck and causing it to bolt. As the deer ran back down the dirt road, the preacher and his brother jumped into the truck to give chase to the bolting buck.

After ten or fifteen minutes, they looked up and saw the deer standing just staring at them, daring them to take a shot. Rusty urged the preacher to hop out and shoot the deer. Before the preacher could ready his gun to shoot, the deer took two bounds away and stopped to look back at them again.

Rusty took aim on the little deer. He was determined that the deer would not win this round. The adrenaline pumped as Rusty got the deer in his sights. As he breathed and steadied his gun, focusing on the little deer, a dog came out of the woods sending the deer bounding away. Rusty hollered, "Let's go! We will catch him when he crosses that dirt road over there!" As Rusty got into his truck, he pulled his gun in, forgetting to take the primer cap off of his black powder gun. When he went to lay the gun in the floorboard of the pick-up truck, the hammer of the rifle got caught on his hunting coat and popped the primer cap, causing the gun to fire inside the vehicle. A loud explosion, followed immediately by a cloud of burning smoke, filled the cab of the pickup truck.

The preacher spun around in his seat, wheeling toward the door, unsure how much of the motion was because of the force of the gun blast and how much was from sheer instinct to dodge the explosion. The preacher would realize after a moment of shock that his left foot had taken the full brunt of that shot. The cab was encased in smoke and thick with the smell of gunpowder. A shudder of disbelief followed by a feeling of sheer panic washed over Rev. Englewilde, as his ears rang from the aftermath of the shot. Rusty, unaware of the severity of what had just occurred sat stunned in the clearing smoke. Warren's door was still open and he dropped his own gun out onto the grass. The thick white smoke billowed out as he laid down across the seat with his feet hanging out of the open door. As he regained his composure and fought to make sense of what had just happened, Rusty asked, "Are you ok?" to which the preacher replied as calmly as he could, "You shot me, man. Get me to a hospital!" Rusty's first reaction was to ask, "Are you sure?".

"Yeah, man, I'm sure!"

"Well, take your boot off and let's look at it."

"Nope, not taking my boot off! My foot may fall off."

The preacher was using all of his willpower to remain calm. The bullet had passed through his foot and left a hole in the floorboard of the truck. Rev. Englewilde truly thought that his foot had been severed completely from the end of his leg and that it was only being held in place by his mangled, melted, rubber boot. The nearest hospital was 40 miles away. Rusty took off toward West Florida Hospital in his 1975 pickup truck, his top speed peaked at 84 mph. Along the drive, they met five different squad cars, to which they flashed their lights and waved their arms, attempting to get their attention for some police emergency assistance. Not a single officer slowed or looked in their direction. Any other day, they would have been ticketed for reckless driving and speeding, but they were unable to gain any of the attention of the police on patrol that day.

Upon their eventual arrival at the hospital, Rusty looked at his brother and said, "You sit right here. I'll go get you a wheelchair." Rev. Englewilde, in his quit-wit replied, "I can't walk so I guess I will be right here." It seemed like Rusty was gone for an eternity. He could have been gone three minutes or thirty, but to the preacher, it was an eternity. He sat there in the cab of that truck, parked in front of the emergency entrance, fearing the worst. He had yet to look at the mangled remains of his foot. He felt himself getting weak and pale as the adrenaline began to dissipate in his body. He had not allowed himself to let his leg drop. Rather he had held it up, not allowing the foot to touch the floor below. After such a long time in that position, his hip was beginning to cramp. He couldn't move it and was scared to try. Across the driveway, an ambulance was parked and the EMT workers who were attending to the supplies took notice of the pale preacher sitting listlessly in the cab. They rushed over to ask if he was ok. Rev. Englewilde responded, "Well, my brother shot me and he went inside to get a wheelchair but he hasn't come back yet." When the paramedic looked down and saw the bottom of the boot missing with blood and tendons hanging out from the bottom of his foot, he turned to get his partner and they scurried to attend to the preacher. They quickly prepped the gurney from their ambulance and helped the preacher onto it and wheeled him into the hospital. As they entered the door, Rusty was coming out with the wheelchair. The preacher flagged his brother down from the gurney to let him know the wheelchair was no longer necessary.

Apparently anytime one appears at the doors of the ER with a gunshot wound, the police are notified immediately. The brothers explained the details of the incident to the medical staff as well as the police. Pain medications were administered to the preacher and every time he awoke another officer was there to question him about the incident. The inquiries were geared around making certain that the shooting had indeed been an accident and not some brotherly quarrel. It was determined that the shot went through just below his ankle, exiting through the bottom of the foot and taking quite a large portion of flesh with it as it exited. Several bones were severed in two. Some were knocked completely out. All in all, he was in the hospital for about three weeks.

On the day that his first child was born, he had been out of the hospital for eight days. He was still in a wheelchair and had a cast from his toes to his hip. Arrangements were made that his wife be placed in a semi private room, she in one bed and the other bed made available for the preacher to stay while visiting his wife and newborn daughter.

When she went into labor, there was a sea of emotions flooding the hearts and minds of that young couple. The arrest of the previous year and all that had transpired because of it was still fresh;

an open wound just beginning to heal. The gunshot wound was also a very literal open wound, causing uncertainty and threatening a complete amputation of the remaining parts of the foot. As the preacher sat in his wheelchair near his wife's head while she labored to deliver their first child, he was reminded of all the events of the past year, all the heartache, all the pain, all the doubt. But he was also reminded of the blessings that come in the darkest of times. The trials they had faced had resulted in stronger faith, stronger relationships, and a deeper appreciation for God's grace and mercy. It was in contemplation of all these things that gave the preacher and his wife comfort as they welcomed into the world their very own Angel.

Just a little over a year after he was initially arrested and three weeks after he had been accidentally shot, the preacher and his wife welcomed their first child into the world - a precious girl with blonde hair and blue eyes. Rev. Englewilde reflected back to all he had gone through in the prior months. He and his wife chose a name for their daughter that could serve as a reminder that God is always watching over us and sends us comfort when we need it. The name they chose was Angelisa Marielle, which is translated to mean "a messenger of God, in the midst of bitter water". Her name was a testament to the grace and mercy God had shown and would continue to show in their lives. Unbeknownst to the preacher, that small child would grow to be one of his biggest fans, holding her daddy in the highest of regards and believing him to be invincible and able to move mountains with his unwavering faith. She would be his best friend in dark times ahead. She would be his helper in the ministry at times. She would grow to be a mother herself and give him grandchildren. She would one day become aware of what her name means and she would try as best she could to live up to its promise. None of these possibilities even entered their minds, as they prayed and praised God over their tiny little miracle - their rainbow at the end of a very dark and trying storm.

Chapter 4

In August of 1982, Rev. Englewilde packed up his meager belongings, his wife, and their young baby girl and took a new pastorate in a small rural community in Mississippi. It was a small, country church in a small, country setting -idyllic even - but little did he know the heartache and pain he would encounter in the years to come as a result of that move. There were many high points that occurred as a result of the move as well. Valley View Baptist Church was home to many good ole boys and their families. While they were accustomed to the regularity of church attendance, they had ideas differing from the preacher concerning evangelism, discipleship, and some of the more basic principles of Christianity. In spite of this, the church saw growth. This growth was immediate and attendance records were set that still stand unmatched to this day.

Sadly, the preacher was met with some occasionally wild and unusual opposition at times. There was one man in particular that really took an interest in driving the poor preacher insane. Larry Lowman was a farmer in the community and had grown to believe the church was somehow his responsibility to police from time to time. He refused to acknowledge the preacher as the leader he was intended to be. Perhaps he resented the preacher's young age, but the preacher believed that Larry's real issue was with the Lord rather than with him personally. Regardless of his reasoning, Larry was a thorn in the preacher's side on more than a few occasions.

The preacher and his small family lived in the cinder block parsonage seated next to the church building itself. This afforded no privacy for the preacher, but his ministry in this church field was his calling so he didn't mind too terribly. What he did mind was parishioners entering his home without announcement or forewarning. So accustomed were these parishioners to running things their own way, they often took large leaps over personal space boundaries. It was revealed during a church business meeting that good, ole Larry had been keeping tabs on the preacher and his family. The sun-hardened farmer stood piously and reported exactly how many lights he'd seen burning in the parsonage at one time, addressing the fact that the only ones living there were the preacher, his wife, and a tiny baby. He proposed there be a change considering the church paid the light bill for the preacher. Actions such as this were typical of Larry. While the other parishioners seemed to be accustomed to his behavior, Rev. Englewilde was not. Nor was he willing to adjust. He saw this as unnecessary opposition over a matter so trivial in comparison to reaching souls and ministering to those in need. To say he was frustrated would be an understatement. There would be many more such business meetings at Valley View during his three and a half years there as pastor.

While Larry definitely served as a thorn in the preacher's side, there were others in the Valley View community who would prove to be a blessing to Rev. Englewilde. One of those individuals was a young man by the name of Paul Amon. He was young and on fire for the Lord and quickly became the preacher's partner in community outreach and prayer. Paul's parents were less than enthusiastic about his newfound friendship with Rev. Englewilde. Often, his parents would refuse to allow him access to the family vehicle, in an effort to limit his time with the preacher and the church, but Paul would simply walk the three miles from his home to the parsonage to meet up with the preacher so they could visit the community together in an effort to bring more souls into the fold. Paul was young and full of zeal. He yearned for the things of the Lord and he desperately wanted to reach his small community for Christ. He wanted to singlehandedly bring revival to his county. Together with Rev. Englewilde, he vowed to re-awaken his part of Mississippi for God. The people within the community, on the other hand, were stubborn people - steeped in their own traditions and comfortable with their level of spirituality. Paul would spend a few years trying tirelessly to win his loved ones for Christ. He met and married a beautiful young girl who also attended Valley View. Rev. Englewilde and his wife proved to be great friends to Paul and his bride Anna. They spent evenings together, playing board games and studying the Bible. Anna was a much-needed friend and helper when the young Mrs. Englewilde gave birth to a second daughter Trinity Reese in the spring Of 1984. When Pastor Englewilde and his young family were called to Allelujah Baptist Church about an hour away, Paul and Anna regularly visited the Englewildes. They grew close to them and were viewed as family. Paul even taught little Angelisa how to tie her shoes as she grew. He surrendered to preach and filled the pulpit for the preacher on occasion. They had formed a life-long bond - a friendship that few get to experience. The two men took mission trips together; they hunted together, fished together, and prayed together. Their friendship, to some, mirrored that of the Biblical Paul and Timothy. They both found common ground in Christ and took pleasure growing and cultivating a friendship rooted in Christ. It didn't hurt that they both had similar humor and personalities as well. Both of their wives would surely roll their eyes in agreement at this summation, be assured.

The preacher had found a kindred spirit in that small, rural Mississippi community - one that would stay true for decades to come. Years later, their friendship would prove to withstand the test of time. Years in which Rev. Englewilde felt his lowest would be the years in which their friendship would be sharpened like iron.

Chapter 5

Allelujah Baptist Church was nestled in a small, rural community-steeped in southern tradition, charm, and prejudice. There were more cows in the county than people. And that's how they liked it. Growing the church would prove difficult because of the proximity to absolutely nowhere convenient. The people were warm and welcoming to Pastor Englewilde and his family. The Tuesday afternoon quilting bee made sure he was fed treats, cakes, and pies regularly. Sandy made the best fried chicken in three counties. Edna made a mean pound cake. Barbara Jean had a secret recipe for the biggest cat-head biscuits the preacher had ever seen. There wasn't a Sunday that went by that they weren't guests at the lunch table of one parishioner or another. Ladies scrambled to be next in line to host the preacher's family for a meal. If Sunday lunch was claimed, they began to request Saturday evening dinners instead. These dinners often occurred at the homes of the younger families with children. The pastor's young daughters played with the other children as the adults mastered Pictionary and Win, Lose, or Draw. With a good mix of older and younger families, the preacher and his wife quickly found a welcome place amongst the congregation of Allelujah Baptist. Everyone in the church was excited as the Englewildes welcomed a son in the fall of

1986. Their family was growing and so were their relationships within the community.

The numbers in attendance improved as well, somehow managing to draw a crowd out of the woods and into the sanctuary every Sunday. Their fifth Sunday singings and dinners-on-the-ground never failed to draw in other parishioners from neighboring churches. Big things were beginning to happen at the little church in the woods. The congregation grew excited. They began to plan Vacation Bible School for the summer. It was quite common in those rural communities for churches to take teams of people to host backyard Bible schools for those kids who may not be able to get rides to the church-hosted VBS week. These backyard Bible schools also provided the opportunity to reach out into the neighboring communities and reach more potential parishioners and souls for Christ.

The congregants of Allelujah Baptist Church eagerly jumped at the opportunity to be a vital part of the summer backyard ministry. One of the deacons gifted the preacher a Ford station wagon to help bring in children to church and VBS. The preacher and his wife used that green wagon to haul people into the neighboring communities for backyard Bible clubs. They used it to drive the children around the dusty farm roads to announce that VBS was coming. It was faithful to carry cookies and Kool-Aid to backyard picnic tables set up under old oak trees to quench the thirst of hungry boys and girls. It was faithful to transport Bibles and Gospel pamphlets to all the low-income communities that neighbored the shadow of the steeple.

When the week came for the church-hosted VBS to occur, that green Ford station wagon was faithful to drive into the poorest of neighboring communities - the one with cinderblock buildings and shotgun sheds that double as housing -and gather 17 boys and girls for VBS. Rev. Englewilde was so excited to be able to utilize this gifted wagon for God's glory. He was on cloud nine as he wound his way along the dusty farm roads with his precious cargo completely filling every possible seat and more in that green wagon. A group of kids this large on the first night of VBS was surely a good sign! He couldn't wait to arrive at the church and see how many children the other church members were able to bring!

As he pulled into the church parking lot and parked in his usual spot near his office door, a couple of deacons glanced his direction and did a double-take. The preacher paid little attention to them as he helped to unload the 17 children from his jam-packed car. When asked later if he noticed the tension then, he doesn't recall. But these kids were much darker in skin pigmentation than any that had ever graced the doorway of Allelujah Baptist Church, a detail that had completely escaped the preacher because, to him, it didn't matter in the slightest.

Unfortunately, this detail did matter very much to the members of his church. It mattered for a few terrible reasons that the Pastor had never before encountered. He had never seen Christians physically turn and shun someone in the doorway of the church before, much less had he seen an adult shun a small child. It was bewildering and shocking to his spirit. He had so looked forward to teaching boys and girls of all backgrounds and ages of the love of Jesus. He thought his congregation had also been looking forward to the opportunity. The reactions he was witnessing alerted him to issues he had yet to even consider. To him, the only thing that mattered was telling them about Jesus.

He was now residing in the very heart of rural Mississippi - known by some as the Klan capital of the South. The people in that region were still neck-deep in southern prejudice and tradition. (Pun very much intended.) They still rallied under sheets in the darkness of a summer night. They still sought vigilante justice. And even though it was the late 1980s, they still burned the occasional cross.

By the time the preacher returned to the parsonage that night from delivering all of those children back to their respective homes, his phone was ringing off the hook. When he finally reached the phone to answer it, threats were whispered over the line. Vile, dark threats stemming directly from the Ku Klux Klan spewed from the phone receiver as if the Devil himself had dialed the extension. Pastor Englewilde already had had a run in with the Klan, but this time they were threatening him rather than incriminating him. This time was way scarier because it involved the safety of his family, already sleeping for the night. As the voice on the phone threatened him for bringing "those kids" to church, Rev. Englewilde summoned the courage to respond. "If you so much as drive by and light a cigarette in my yard, you'll be picking buckshot out of your backside for the next week!" He slammed the phone down and retrieved his shotgun from the closet.

The calls continued for a few days. Refusing to be defeated, the preacher continued to go and try to bring the children to VBS. But, after the second night, word had gotten around and the parents of the children no longer thought it safe to send their young ones to VBS. By the end of the week, the tension began to dissipate but the preacher continued to guard his sleeping family with a loaded shotgun for several more weeks. He had his wife, two daughters, and newborn son Jacob to protect.

The week after VBS, the man who had gifted Rev. E the station wagon called and requested a visit. The preacher drove the car to the visit and made pleasantries with Mr. Turner. After a few moments, Mr. Turner got right down to the matter at hand. He expressed his disappointment in the pastor for using that car to transport *those* kids. Rev. Englewilde allowed Mr. Turner to say his piece - his racist, bigoted piece - then slowly withdrew the keys from his pocket and laid them on the table in front of Mr. Turner. The preacher stood, looked Mr. Turner square in the eye and said, "You gave me that car to bring souls to Christ. I did just that. God doesn't see color because all souls are equal and are in equal need of salvation. If I can't use this car to bring souls to Christ, I don't want it." As he turned to leave, Mr. Turner stopped him. "Pastor, that's not what I meant. . . I just meant. . . Don't bring them to the church. Use the car to go to them all you want. Just don't bring them to our church."

Rev. Englewilde, with tears in his eyes, just shook his head and walked out the door. He walked all the way home, contemplating along the way how someone could possibly be so cold and callous toward anyone in need of God's love and mercy. He hobbled along that country road, on his crippled foot, praying to God for the strength to deal with this hard and callous people. He had been called here to reach this community for Christ and that meant the entire community and not just a select group. He struggled to understand such bias and how it could stem from so-called Christians.

The members of his congregation were quick to give generously to mission endeavors and to send money to foreign countries, yet they were unwilling to reach the poor souls who resided in their own community and attended the same schools as their own kids. They only seemed interested in reaching those with whom they'd never actually made contact. This saddened the preacher. It grieved his spirit. In the months to follow, the church would rally together and raise funds to send him on a mission trip to India. Perhaps, this was a way to make amends with him for their behavior during VBS; probably not, though. It was more likely a way to appease their guilty consciences. Within a few months, they had raised enough to send Rev. Englewilde on the planned trip with a few other preachers, his friend Rev. Townsend being one of those. This trip would hold a world of excitement, spiritual warfare like he'd never before seen, and experiences that would provide a lifetime of stories and intrigue.

Chapter 6

January 1990 would grow to be a monumental month in the life of Rev. Englewilde. He had been at Allelujah Baptist Church for a few years and he had made some progress in teaching his congregation some important truths from the Bible regarding discipleship and ministry. There had been no more incidents like the VBS fiasco. Things had calmed down and he had found his groove. In the weeks prior to the trip, his health had given him a scare. Not only had he had to go Houston for more surgeries on his foot, but he had also begun to cough and struggle to speak at times. He suffered a sore throat always. His style of dynamic preaching was significantly more than monotone, leading to the eventual stripping out of his vocal cords. Fearing that he may permanently damage his vocal cords, the doctors put him on voice rest. Imagine, a man whose life is speaking, being told not to speak! For six weeks! He restricted himself to speaking only in the pulpit. He made no announcements, nor did he sing during services, which quite possibly was a blessing to his congregants. He carried a notepad around with him in order to communicate with his family. For six long, silent weeks, the preacher had rested his voice and bit his tongue to keep from commenting on anything and everything around him. He was as good a patient as he could possibly be, in preparation for the mission trip to India.

Finally, his vocal cords had healed and the voice ban was lifted by his doctors. He set out for a two-week mission trip to India with several preachers. There they met up with local pastors who would take turns hosting the American preachers and would provide them with help interpreting the varying languages of the region. The call to spread the Gospel of Christ would be difficult to fulfill in this land that worshipped over a million gods. Convincing them to worship Jesus Christ would be no problem. Convincing these people to turn from their millions of false gods to serve the ONE TRUE GOD would be an almost insurmountable challenge. After a short, futile attempt to recover from the jet lag, the group of preachers all headed out to preach at various local churches in the region.

Rev. Englewilde's voice was still recovering but he was anxious for the opportunity to preach the Word of God in this foreign land. The first few days were a blur. They spent their days preaching and traveling and preaching some more. Many Indian natives were gathered in churches all over the region for a chance to meet the American preachers, who stood a full head taller than the average Indian inhabitant and whose skin shone white in the moonlight. Rev. Englewilde encountered a woman who had walked several miles, days in advance, just to be present in the service nearest her village. Rev. Englewilde's interpreter pointed her out to him before the service began. When the preaching service had ended and their time of prayer had closed, the people milled about and filed out of the little dirt-floored church building. All exited but this one, elderly lady.

Rev. Englewilde noticed a commotion near where the woman had been seated. The muddled voices were all speaking an Indian dialect, but he had no way of knowing what they were saying until the interpreter came to his side. The woman had passed away during the service. Most likely, she had succumbed to the intense heat and had suffered lethal heat exhaustion, but they were surrounded by villages who strongly believed in spirits and signs. Rev. Englewilde knew these were a people of superstition and feared they may equate this woman's death to the God of the American preachers. Immediately, he began to pray, "Lord, you are the God of all creation. You know all before it comes to pass. Lord, if this woman dies here, in this Christian service, the pagans will be convinced that our God did it. Lord, we know you are mighty!" As he prayed, the woman stirred! She sat up, looked around, then stood and staggered toward the exit. The preacher stood, amazed and in awe, as he watched her slowly shuffle out and into the crowd that had gathered just outside the door. Rev. Englewilde's heart soared and his mind raced as he processed what had just happened. All of those who had gathered around that woman's body had declared her dead since she had lain unresponsive for over an hour, yet she stood and walked away on her own! How mightily his God had shown himself that day! The excitement of that event carried the team on to their next speaking engagement a few hours away.

The days were long and the roads were rough. While he ministered to these strangers in a foreign land, his heart ached to be at home with his wife and three young children, especially at night in the darkness of a foreign land. The pressures of the pastorate had begun to threaten the peace and civility of his home. Long hours away visiting shut-ins and ill congregants in the hospital kept him from being home with his young family. He was fiercely dedicated to his calling to minister to others. His time in India was a spiritual rejuvenation that ignited a new flame for his ministry. The wonders and terrors he would witness would change him. But his wife was at home with the kids during those weeks. She did not receive that same rejuvenation that her husband did. Instead, she was holding down the home front with three young children. There was an unravelling that had begun somewhere in their marriage – a slow, methodic, almost microscopic erosion of the bond between husband and wife. It began so inconsequentially small that neither noticed it for quite some time.

One of the scariest places the preacher found himself was deep within the Lambada tribes. He and Rev. Townsend were the first white men to ever visit the Lambadas. Uncertain of what to expect, the men placed their full trust in God. Only He could ensure their safety. There was very sparse electricity running to this village. One 60-watt lightbulb provided a glow in the street. A similar light illuminated the pulpit of the open-air space they would be using as a church. This tribe was steeped in their own ritualistic religion, complete with a village witch-doctor. The witch doctor was less than enthused to have these strange white men speaking in his village about a "one true God". He had sent word to several villagers instructing them to have nothing to do with the white strangers or their "new god". The preachers arrived in the village at dusk. They walked through the village with their interpreter, taking note that the huts were small enough that even Rev. Townsend could see over them and he was not nearly as tall as Rev. Englewilde. They walked cautiously as their eyes met with an increasing number of tribal villagers whose curiosity could not keep them from the pale strangers before them. A crowd quickly began to form, encircling the preachers. Never before had the people of this village seen the milky white skin of an American. Their children were wide-eyed, half with fear and half with intrigue. The crowd followed and grew as the preachers walked to the dimly lit pavilion in which they were to hold the service. Many of the villagers piled into the space. One of those in the crowd was the wife of the aforementioned witch doctor. This was a fact that the preachers could not have possibly known, and it went unknown until the service was in full swing. As Rev. Englewilde began to present the Gospel to this crowd of Lambada natives, a loud commotion got his attention. A wild looking man with a large staff came thundering into the crowd, stormed straight to a woman situated in the front of the building and commenced to dragging her out of the service by her hair as she wailed and screamed into the night. It was later confirmed that the man had been the witch doctor and the woman, his wife. Her screams were heard until they finally faded into the distance. Presenting the Gospel became an even greater challenge with the fear of what had just happened still clung to the air.

The lack of screams rang louder than the actual screams had. Rev. Englewilde attempted to recollect his thoughts and got back to the message at hand while Rev. Townsend fervently prayed for the Spirit to defeat whatever wickedness still lingered. As he prayed, Rev. Englewilde preached. As the message went on, another sound began to perforate the darkness. It was the howl of a dog. Dogs, in the tribal interiors of India, are not kept as house pets. They are mostly wild.

As the dog's howl got increasingly closer, other dogs joined in. They began not only to howl but to growl. As this growling pack of wild dogs drew nearer to the service, the lights in the village went black. No light could be seen anywhere. In the pitch darkness of a hidden village deep in the heart of the jungles of India, Rev. Englewilde relied solely on the Holy Spirit to calm his nerves as he continued delivering his message of the Gospel to these people who so desperately needed to hear it. The growling dogs encircled the place and threatened to devour any who dared to cross them.

All the while, Rev. Townsend was on his knees in earnest prayer. The dogs snarled and slobbered ferociously as they walked methodically around and around the gathering of people. Suddenly, all at once, the dogs ceased their growling and the lights once again dimly illuminated the night. A calm came over the place. As Rev. Englewilde closed his message, many began to stir from their seats and come forward to accept the God who had calmed the night's terrors. There was a spiritual war taking place in the darkness that night, a war whose details we mortals may never uncover, but in the light of a 60-watt bulb, many Lambada villagers accepted the one true God and escaped the power of the witch doctor.

When the preachers were safe and alone once again, they were able to reflect upon the happenings of the evening with almost disbelief. Had they really just witnessed that themselves? How mighty God's hand is when the people of God pray in earnest and believe in

His might! How miraculous - and downright terrifying - the night had been! And the trip was only half over. The miracles they would witness were only just beginning.

When they continued their travel into more civilized towns, the crowds grew larger. Services often ended with many lining up to meet the American preachers and to have them pray for varying illnesses and family members. One lady in particular would prove very memorable, second only to the woman who had sprung back to life days earlier. She approached the preachers in tears and was speaking rather urgently and pointing to her chest. Rev. Englewilde attempted to understand but his interpreter had wandered out of earshot and was helping Rev. Townsend.

The woman grabbed Rev. Englewilde's hand and placed it on her chest, where he felt a mass the side of a grapefruit. He could only assume it to be cancer or some sort of tumor. Having gained some understanding of her situation, he began to pray for healing. He prayed earnestly and with a faith he had not felt before he had embarked on the trip. He had seen things that had grown his faith exponentially. As he prayed for the woman to receive healing, he felt something begin to happen. The mass under his hand was changing. It was *shrinking* as he prayed! By the time he had finished his prayer, the woman was excitedly chattering in a language he could not understand – but there was no mistaking what she was feeling! She was as amazed at what had happened as he was himself. To God be the glory!!! She had been healed before his very eyes, under his very hand! Such miracles were surely a blessing to behold. These were miracles of Biblical proportions. Oh, if only the people of God in America had faith like he was seeing in this foreign land!

As he rode this spiritual high, he could not wait to get back to his family and tell them all that he had experienced. Not only were the services an adventure in and of themselves, but the entire trip had held new experiences.

Some of the native families had hosted the preachers in their homes for meals. Having heard that they were from the American South and loved fried chicken, one of the families prepared a meal of fried chicken for them to enjoy. It should be noted that the average citizen of a third world country has never before tasted fried chicken. There are no KFC restaurants in the interior jungles of India. They can't just run and by some butter flavored Crisco from a supermarket. The preachers sat down to two chicken legs, dripping with grease. The grease they had used to fry up these little legs was fish oil, because that is what they had in abundance. When they bit into the chicken, the meat itself was green. It can only be assumed that they killed their chicken a few days too early in anticipation of the arrival of the

Americans. So, the two preachers graciously ate their green, fish-flavored chicken while their hosts watched on in glee, proud to have been able to provide the meal for the Americans. As they slowly and methodically chewed, they prayed for the very best outcome, hoping not to become violently ill.

They would later remember this to be one of the better meals of their visit. This, in itself, was yet one more miracle that they witnessed on the life-changing trip. The fact that they could consume the things they were presented and not suffer food poisoning or worse was nothing short of miraculous. Another family who hosted them offered them a refreshing beverage. The family was one of few in the village who owned their own goat, from which they could collect milk for making cheese and butter. The preachers were each given a fresh cup of goat's milk, still warm from the teat.

Rev. Englewilde and Rev. Townsend took their cups and looked down to see a film of cream, tiny bugs, and debris that lined the surfaces of their drinks. Knowing that to refuse the drink would be an intense insult to their hosts, Rev. Englewilde stuck his finger into the cup, withdrawing it along with a string of stuff from the surface of that milk. He quickly slung it off his finger and onto the ground and took the goat's milk in one shot. Rev. Townsend, impressed with the quick thoughts and actions of his friend, took a different approach. While the host's back was turned, he quickly switched his full cup for Rev. Englewilde's empty one and exclaimed, "Wow! That was good! Brother Warren, you got to try this!" Rev. Englewilde grimaced as he saw what his sneaky friend had just done. He knew he would now have to drink another cup of the warm, gritty milk. The host's attention was turned to him now in anticipation, pleased to have provided them with such a treat. He could not use his finger to remove the film from the top as he had done before. Not under the scrutiny of his gracious host. He managed to grit his teeth and strain most of the bugs and debris from the milk with his teeth and he shot irritated looks at his friend, who quietly chuckled at his discomfort. Rev. Englewilde waited throughout the afternoon for his stomach to revolt, but it never did. Yet another miracle on the foreign soil of India.

On one of the last nights of their trip, the preachers were picked up by a cab and were to be driven through the wee hours of the morning into the city of New Delhi. It was well after midnight before they were able to get free from the crowd at their scheduled service and get into the cab. They were exhausted from the heat and the rigid schedule. Rev. Townsend took full advantage of the dark night and quickly succumbed to slumber in the back seat of the cab. Rev. Englewilde leaned his head against the window of his car door and attempted to quiet his mind from the excitement of the trip and the bumpy, backseat ride. He had almost completely fallen asleep when the cab hit a particularly terrible bump and his door was jarred open. He groped to find something to cling to as he fell headfirst out of the door, fighting to hang on as his eyes registered how close he had come to the ground outside the careening car. He still managed to keep his body in the car, centering his weight in the seat, and he struggled to keep a grip on the seat as he fought to get his head and shoulders back in the car. His free hand flailed desperately to grab the car door and get it shut. The car never slowed. The driver never hit the brakes. In fact, the car seemed to be gaining speed. It all happened so fast but seemed to also drag on for an infinity. At last, he was able to clamor back upright and get the door latched back in the closed position. Breathless, he sat staring around him in disbelief. He glanced over at Rev. Townsend, still sleeping in complete oblivion. His eyes caught the rearview mirror and in it, he saw the reflection of evil itself. The cab driver sat glaring at him through the mirror. Only his eyes glowed in the pitch black of the starless night. A low, malevolent chuckle rumbled from the man's throat. A chill passed over the preacher as he began to realize what was at work here.

He was unable to sleep any more. Instead, he sat, fervently praying for God's mighty hand to continue to intervene. Also, he hoped his friend would awaken soon. The sun began to appear on the horizon, shedding some light onto the very, very dark night. With that light, the evil seemed to evaporate from the atmosphere. Rev. Townsend stirred awake in the morning sun. They were nearing their destination. He looked over and saw something in Rev. Englewilde's face. Though he didn't yet know the details, he knew a great battle had taken place. Rev. Englewilde's eyes reflected an exhaustion that only came from waging spiritual warfare. They also shone with a newfound confidence in God.

Chapter 7

When Rev. Englewilde returned from India, he had a newfound zeal for the Gospel. He had witnessed firsthand how mightily his God worked. He wanted his own community to experience the sort of blessing that total faith in God could bring. His excitement was not always matched. At home, his own spiritual rejuvenation had not been mirrored in the lives of his wife and kids. They had not travelled to the foreign field with him. They had not shared the experiences he had encountered. For them, life had been only more difficult with his absence. It was two weeks of revival for him, but for them it was simply a time of difficulty without his presence. The kids had missed him. They had cried every night, unable to talk to him on the phone. They were too young still to fully comprehend the passage of time. The oldest, Angelisa, was 7, followed by her 5-year-old sister Trinity Reese and their 2-year-old brother Jacob. All they had known was that they missed their daddy very much and their mommy seemed to be sad as well. Certainly, the age of the children compounded the stress of being the only parent for the duration of the mission trip. What had served as a time of rejuvenation for him had been a much different experience for his wife. The small ravel in the thread of their marriage was quickly becoming a tear. He didn't know how to fix it. He didn't understand her distance, her lack of excitement. He was reeling on the heels of an incredible experience and he had no way to relay that and make a connection with his wife. The ministry had begun to feel like it was only his, when it had been *theirs* for so long.

He felt the Lord calling him to a change. It came in the form of a pulpit committee. They approached him from a fledgling church on the Mississippi Gulf Coast. Once much larger, the existing congregants wanted to breathe new life into the immense facilities they owned. They wanted to see God renew a work in the once thriving house of worship. Rev. Englewilde prayed and contemplated the call to be their pastor for many weeks. He and his wife spent many a night discussing the option and they finally settled it in their hearts. It was God's will for them to move on. Their little family seemed to thrive in the new place. The church's vast property included several apartments at the back of the property, making it an ideal place for the family to reside. The pastor was on-call 24 hours a day. He lived for the opportunity to serve and minister to this new community. The opportunity to aid Rev. Englewilde in service for the community became obvious to Paul Amon, who had recently had a son with his wife Anna. They moved into one of the provided apartments and quickly went to work inviting people to services and building up a bus ministry. The two families seemed to be a dream team for the Lord. The church began to grow exponentially. Souls were saved. One bus route quickly became two.

Two busses became four. They painted that first bus Grabber Blue with Pigeon Blood Red lettering. It captivated the attention of everyone in town.

One of the women that the bus attracted seemed more than a little peculiar. She was friendly and conversational before the services began. She seated herself toward the back of the sanctuary. She was by herself in attendance. During the song service, they had a time of fellowship in which congregants went around greeting each other and welcoming visitors to the service. Several went by her pew to shake her hand and welcome her. She was polite and congenial to all who greeted her. But something changed in her countenance when the preaching service began. As soon as the Word of God was opened and read, she began to thrash about in her seat. She swatted at her face as if she were fighting a swarm of bees. She made such a commotion that Rev. Englewilde found himself somewhat distracted in the pulpit. He struggled to stay on point throughout his sermon because of the disturbance in the woman's pew. After the service, she had disappeared by the time he made his way to the foyer. But she had left her information on a visitor's card, so he and his wife made plans to visit with her in her home later that week. The visit began just as her visit to the church had. She was friendly and welcoming, inviting the couple into her home for sweet tea. They began to talk about church and her background. After a few minutes of small talk, the preacher opened his Bible to share a word of scripture with her. At that precise moment, she threw herself to the floor. The dish towel she had been holding in her hands was now being rung and stretched as she writhed in the floor, covering her face. Shocked, Rev. Englewilde gave pause to his reading and glanced over at his wife, who was frozen in disbelief. Rev. Englewilde held his place in his Bible with his finger and closed it to check on the woman. As soon as the book was shut, she sat up, wiped her face clean, and sat composed in the chair as if nothing had happened. Once again, the preacher opened his Bible to continue. As soon as he did, she threw herself in the floor again and commenced to writhing, as if the very words spoken were acid in her ears. As his wife sat watching it all in horror, the preacher felt he had a good idea of what was going on. He had seen demon possession and demonic activity in India. It wasn't something he would soon forget. He closed his Bible once more and she, once again, regained her composure as if nothing unusual had happened. Just to be sure, he tested his theory once more. He began reading again as he prayed, both for the situation and for an escape from this bizarre visit. The scene played itself out once again just as it had before. Clearly there was a demonic force at hand that did not wish for this woman to hear the Gospel. When she was once again composed, they thanked her for her hospitality and excused themselves from her home. Rev.

Englewilde left experiencing an array of emotions. He was more than a little excited. It was like a soldier being sent to the front line and seeing real action for the first time in a long time. He also felt an overwhelming concern for this woman's soul, which seemed locked in the clutches of the devil himself, and she seemingly had no idea. She never once seemed even to be aware of her fits in the floor. He was also a little fearful for his wife, who had never encountered anything like what they had just witnessed and still seemed frozen with terror or shock long after they had left the home. The woman did return for another visit on the following Wednesday night and asked to meet with the pastor and his wife for counseling following the service. The three talked for over an hour in his office. A few days later, she called to talk once again over the phone. He began to witness to her and share the Gospel but she, or something in her, fought the topic. She cried and she brought up past issues from her life and she danced around the conversation to keep the focus off of the Gospel. Rev. Englewilde could tell this was not the characteristically charming woman who had seemed so inquisitive when she had sat in counseling. Her personality was much altered due to whatever demonic force had taken over her mind. Now, it is important to note here that the church and the pastor's home both shared the same phone line, which the pastor had tied up on this call. Unbeknown to him at the time, while he was talking to this woman on the phone in his office, the phone was ringing in his home. After several rings, Angelisa saw that no one else was going to answer, so she answered it. She had been learning phone etiquette in her fifth-grade class and was excited to get to put what she had learned into practice. When she lifted the receiver and chimed "Englewilde Residence", she was disappointed to find here were no voices on the other end of the line; just the sound of someone playing the tune Mary Had a Little Lamb on the phone keys. It was an odd call. She listened for a few seconds, tried to get a reply when she repeatedly answered "Hello, hello?", then hung up. Later, when her daddy finally came home from his church office, she told him about the call. "That's impossible, Angelisa", he said, "I've been on the phone the entire night. I just hung up and walked over here a couple minutes ago." She relayed again her experience and what she had heard over the phone line - the same phone line he had had tied up for the past hour. He instructed her not to answer the phone anymore for a while. He didn't want to scare her, but he also didn't want her exposed to whatever demonic activity may be present. The experience was seemingly harmless but alarming all at once. Twice more, visits were made to this woman's home, but by different congregants. They attempted to reach her for the Lord, but odd happenings always transpired. She even called one of the men who visited her in the middle of the night one night, upsetting his wife in the process. Everything about the woman was a mysterious oddity.

It was determined that they would not compel her to visit the church again. Her presence was a disruption in the services. It was an unnecessary excitement that could potentially put others at risk. Her behavior was erratic upon any mention of Christ or scripture.

She was one in a million. Not all who came acted demon possessed. That was a rarity. Within the first 18 months of his pastorate there, Rev. Englewilde saw the church become the fastest growing church on the Mississippi gulf coast. He had an ever-expanding ministry. The local military base meant there were always new faces coming into town, many of them finding their way to services after being invited by someone in the congregation to visit. There was a spiritual awakening taking place. The entire congregation seemed to buzz with the excitement. Paul and Abby had begun to feel burdened for the mission field and had been earnestly seeking the Lord's direction. They announced in one Sunday evening service that God was calling them to the Philippines. Everyone rejoiced, especially Rev. Englewilde. He had always felt a deep, brotherly bond with Paul. He burst with righteous pride when he learned that God would be using Paul at such magnitude. He would go on to reach hundreds, possibly thousands, in his ministry abroad. Rev. Englewilde had mentored him for years and had seen him grow in the nurture and grace of the Lord. He had ministered alongside him in prisons and communities all across

Mississippi. Now, he would soon see his friend embark on a new journey of ministry, one in which he could not join him. He vowed to support his friend in any way. Rev. Englewilde was soaring on a spiritual high - a high that would soon come plummeting down with great and rapid force.

It was a Tuesday; just a run-of-the-mill Tuesday with very little in the way of consequence. It tends to be that way. Days of little to no importance suddenly become thrust into our memory forever with just one event. It would be a Tuesday he would never forget, forever etched into his mind. The day it all disappeared. To say it was without warning would be unfair and untrue. But it is possible he didn't see the warning signs at first, though the signs had been there. He had been immersed in his ever-growing ministry. This church wasn't nestled in the woods like the others he had pastored. It was in a community way more populated than previous communities in which he had pastored. More population meant more congregants. There were more infirmed to visit, more shut-ins; more first-time visitors to the church meant more follow-up visits. This had equated to earlier mornings and later evenings. Without meaning to, he had neglected to give the proper attention to those waiting at home for him.

He was repairing a bookshelf in his office on that fateful Tuesday afternoon, manual labor he didn't regularly participate in, but it was an easy enough fix and he felt confident he could handle it. Busily at work, he almost didn't notice her standing there. He glanced up at the door. His wife stood at the threshold, seeming hesitant to enter. He stopped the rotation of the circular saw and removed his safety glasses. In the instant that he began to greet her, he met her eyes. There was a resolve there that he hadn't seen before; also, sadness. His heart flip-flopped as he took half a step toward her. She met his gaze with an icy glare. Her voice, when she spoke, was masked with determination, detached from her emotions. She flatly told him she had met with a lawyer. She couldn't do it any longer. She was leaving. She had already taken half of the money in their joint account. She had already arranged to go stay with her sister. She had already worked everything out. He never had a chance to even take a breath and reply. Before he could register all that she had said, she was gone - disappeared from the doorway as quickly as she had appeared. A part of him wanted to believe he had imagined it all. But his heart knew better. He stood there, reeling, as his shattered heart splintered in multi-faceted directions. The realization of what she had told him spread and he began to fully grasp all that the situation now entailed. She was leaving. As good as gone already. Her mind had been made up. Her actions had already showed her resolve. She wasn't going back on it now and he knew it. He also knew what it meant for him. He was losing his wife. What would become of his children? He would now lose his ministry. No one in his circle of peers would ever accept a preacher whose wife had left. A pastor was to be the ruler of his home, the keeper of his wife. But he couldn't keep her. He couldn't force her to stay and he didn't know how to convince her. He had failed in that aspect. She was gone. At some point their ministry had become only his. The trials had been too much and she had not experienced the spiritual rejuvenation that he had felt in India. She had begun to feel isolated and alone in the fishbowl life they lived. He had failed to notice it at first and, when he finally did take notice, he had lacked the ability to remedy the divide between them. She had been gone in her own heart and mind for quite some time. Now she was physically removing herself from the marriage. No longer would it be a secret problem for them to deal with privately. His failures. Her failures. Their failures. They were all being forced into the light now. There was no going back. He felt the soul-crushing weight of her decision. He saw all the flaws in their 15-year marriage and every way he could have fixed them, all in that moment - and all too late. They had taken the kids to Disney just a couple months prior, as a kind of last-ditch effort at repairing their marriage. It had not worked. At least the kids had seemed to enjoy themselves and had not noticed the tension between their parents. It wasn't always so easy to conceal the tension. Their oldest was 11 now and she picked up on a lot of cues. She heard the muted arguing behind closed doors. She had learned to keep her younger siblings entertained and distracted when necessary. Now, he would have to figure out his next step. God had called him to pastor. This seemed impossible now. He would have to find a way to tell the kids what was going on. He feared this would forever crush their innocence. For the moment, he still stood shell-shocked and immensely alone in his office as the sun set in the evening and the darkness closed in all around him.

He resigned from his position as pastor the following Sunday. There were many who shook their heads in disbelief. His family had appeared to be flawless to those whose only glimpse was on Sunday mornings. So polished and put together. How could the pastor and his wife be having problems? They always wore matching clothes and stood happily together as they greeted parishioners following the services. Many offered sympathies. Most were confused. The pastor's family was supposed to be above reproach. They were shocked to find the fallacy of this supposition. Within the following few weeks, he had arranged to move his belongings to his parent's house in his home state of Florida. His wife had set out to begin her new life in Texas. He had the kids in the interim. He began to build a framework to a new type of life; being unable to pastor left him flailing for meaning in all this chaos. The first few weeks were rough. He fought back tears when in the presence of his kids. He held back from telling his parents all that had transpired in his marriage. His parents remained in a state of shock, not understanding what had happened. They never even had a clue that trouble was brewing. They wished they could help. Silently, he suffered as he tried to make sense of it himself. He and his estranged wife were from the same hometown. She came in to visit her parents a couple of months after everything had fallen apart. She called ahead, expressing an interest in taking the children for dinner. Of course, he obliged, knowing the kids had been missing their mother. They were very excited to see her after such a long separation. When she arrived, they hugged their daddy and eagerly greeted their mother with open arms. They jumped into her car, what once had been their family car just months earlier, and headed off to dinner. Some hours later, Rev. Englewilde heard his parents' phone ring in the other room. He was immediately called to the receiver where he heard his estranged wife's voice from the other end of the line. Her words were like mud in his ears. He could not make sense of what she was saying. He slammed the phone back down, shaking his head in an effort to clear his thoughts. Try as he may, he could not make sense of what he had just heard. "She has taken the kids" was all he could croak out as he collapsed in sobs. Dinner had been a ploy. She had devised a plan to get physical possession of the kids. From there, she would seek full custody. She was already across two state lines. There was nothing he could do. His already splintered world was now completely shattered.

Chapter 8

He felt as though he was walking around without a heart beating inside his chest. Not only had his ministry life come to a screeching halt, but he found himself suddenly lacking activity at home as well. He was lost. Free time had never been something he had much of and for good reason. Idleness drove him crazy. He took a job at Wal-Mart, working night shifts and overtime whenever possible. He had visitation with his kids two weekends a month and he was determined not to miss those visits, even though it meant driving 8 hours one-way just to take them for breakfast. He did it, too. He burned the candle at both ends, sleeping when he could, but never missing an opportunity to see his children. There were many trips spent along the I-10 corridor, many prayer sessions along those miles. He learned to tolerate country music since it was the only guaranteed radio entertainment along the stretch of interstate between Florida and Texas. The divorce was finalized a few months later and the kids had all begun to attend school in their new home with their mother.

It was a difficult adjustment for them all. It was mandated in the state of Mississippi, where they had filed for divorce, that the children were free to choose who they wished to live with upon their twelfth birthday. As soon as she was free to choose, his oldest daughter chose to move in with him. But Angelisa was forced to wait.

Her birthday occurred in the spring semester of a school year, so it was decided by both parents that she would finish the school year at her current school. By the time the summer approached, her transition was put off yet again due to her mother remarrying. She was to be in the wedding along with her two siblings and her new step-siblings. She moved in with her daddy the day after her mommy remarried. Rev. Englewilde and his daughter became an inseparable duo. They prayed nightly for the other two children, often crying and pleading for God to reunite them as soon as possible. The day-to-day life was difficult for them. Planning anything seemed like they were having too much fun without the others. The only anticipation they could enjoy was the anticipation of the next visit.

Rev. Englewilde was offered a position as song leader and minister of youth in a small country church, which held their meetings in a barn. They only averaged about 23 people, but it gave the preacher a sense of spiritual purpose again. He was honored that someone would entrust him with a staff position considering his current state of marriage, or the lack thereof. He had prayed about it and gained peace in taking the position. He met a very nice group of people that welcomed him and his daughter and treated them like family. When Trinity Reese and Jacob came to visit that summer, they arranged for a trip to Disney World. A very generous benefactress paid for the preacher to take his kids along with a group of teens to Orlando. It was a much-needed respite for the family that had experienced such turmoil and uncertainty over the preceding months. He took the opportunity to spend as much quality time as he could with his three kids. There were now such few opportunities to have them all gathered together. They made the most of it. He even went bungee-jumping for the sheer amusement of his children, who all squealed and cheered with delight as he plunged through the air! In that moment, he was their hero. In reality, he was always their hero, but he felt it that night. He knew that the hope of the future shone bright in the faces of his children. They were his hope. He would never give up on them. He resolved to fight until he had them all back, under his protective eye.

In all, it would take him two years and a firecracker lawyer to convince a judge to give him physical custody. He continued working at Wal-Mart for a while until a janitorial position became available with another company. The new job allowed him the flexibility to visit his kids in Texas in the interim of custody disputes. There were no more night shifts with that job. He worked there for a while, spending his weekends off work traveling to see Trinity Reese and Jacob in Texas with Angelisa riding shotgun and helping him stay awake. All the while, they prayed. God heard the prayers of the preacher and his young daughter and granted him a unique opportunity. He was offered a position as Principal of a church school in Louisiana in the fall of 1995. The new position had multifaceted blessings. For one, it was several hours closer to his two younger children. Rev. Englewilde and his daughter made the transition, still continuing the fight for custody of the other two children. He had always wanted to start a Christian school, but had never felt led to do so at any of the churches he had pastored. This new opportunity was a dream come true for him, second only to the pulpit itself. He threw himself into the job and all that it entailed.

Most days, he and Angelisa arrived at the school by 6:30 a.m. and did not leave until well into the evening. His daughter stuck by his side through every early morning, through every basketball practice, and through every late afternoon detention session. It was easier when they stayed busy. The alternative reminded them that their family was not whole. Through all the prayer and special Bible study time with her daddy, Angelisa gained the most precious clarity regarding her eternity. Just a few weeks shy of her 13th birthday, she ran to the altar one Sunday morning with tears flooding her cheeks and accepted Jesus Christ as her Savior. This was, perhaps, the largest blessing to come from taking the new position at Dusty Road Christian School.

By the spring of 1996, custody had been granted in his favor and, for him at least, his family felt more complete. Angelisa started high school that fall and his other two children, Trinity Reese and Jacob, integrated fairly easily into their new surroundings and home. Jacob, being only 9, missed his mother immensely at times. Moms have a special bond with their boys by nature and he had developed a special closeness with her in the time she had had custody. He took the transition a little harder than his older sisters, who had always rivaled for their daddy's attention. Girls tend to do that. But despite the difficulty of the situation, they all transitioned well and enjoyed their time in their new home in Louisiana. Jacob and Trinity Reese had become very good at playing basketball out in the big city suburbs with their mother. They reveled in their new school setting and enjoyed the all-access basketball court afforded to them by their dad's job. This, too, proved to only be a temporary dwelling.

In March 1997, Rev. Englewilde was offered a pastorate in south Alabama, a place he had always vowed to retire to someday. After four years away from the pulpit, God was giving him the chance to pastor again. He sought counsel from his pastor and pastor's wife. He had always held the same belief that his preaching acquaintances held: divorced men were not to pastor. But, God Himself had called him to preach when he was merely 15 years old. Who was he to argue with God Almighty? God had known when He had called Him that he would one day face the messiness and disarray of divorce, yet He had still placed that call on his life.

The church in question was the smallest congregation he had ever pastored. In fact, they were less a congregation and more a mere handful. They contacted him in hopes that he could come and help them regrow. The existing building had no real congregation to speak of. It had once been a thriving part of the community, but a previous pastor had made some rather poor life choices and had driven the church into the ground. There was a mortgage on the property and a few elderly members of the community had been fighting with all they had to keep it from defaulting. They had been meeting by candle light, with lay preachers from the community providing sermons and devotions as their schedules permitted. Rev. Englewilde prayed in earnest and sought counsel from his pastor, his parents, and his friends. He came out of those prayer sessions with peace, knowing that God wanted him in Alabama.

An added bonus was that his hometown was less than an hour's drive from the church. It would almost be like coming home for him. He had even pastored in the same building briefly when he had first begun his ministry at eighteen years old. While the church name and denomination had changed quite a few times over the years, the building was much the same. The people who gathered there had decided to name it what it had once been called: Country Road Baptist Church. One or two of his previous congregants still resided in the community some 15 or so years later. One family had maintained contact with him over the years and offered his family a place to stay until Rev. Englewilde could find and purchase a home for himself and his family. The Kindred family had been lifelong friends. He had often made it a point to stop in and visit with them when he found himself travelling through the area. The older couple had children Pastor Englewilde's age and he had enjoyed many hunting and fishing trips with the boys in his younger days. These "kids" all had kids of their own now- with kids the ages of his own kids.

It was unknown to anyone at the time, but one of those adorable little cotton-topped girls would grow to marry his son Jacob one day. But that was not to happen for another two decades. Until then, Lilly would secretly pine over Jacob until the timing was right. She knew when she was 8 years old that she loved him. Her brothers convinced her one day that if she would try out their homemade zip line in the backyard, Jacob would love her forever. That's all it took to convince her to jump up there and try their contraption. Adrenaline coursed through her veins as she climbed to the top and grabbed onto the makeshift handles. A sense of excitement gripped her as she stepped off the ledge. Immediate regret set in when she stepped off the platform and got her hair tangled in the mechanism of the line. Sheer mortification flooded her as she realized Jacob was watching it all. In a way, it worked. It took a while for his silly boy heart to mature, but he did indeed vow to love her forever in June 2013 on the sandy beaches of south Alabama. But, again, there was no way to know any of that in the backyard on that summer afternoon on the zipline.

With this new pastorate came another opportunity. The community had a flourishing Christian school with a growing sports program. Rev. Englewilde's father had known the founding pastor of the church/school years prior. They had shared fellowships together throughout the years. When the preacher inquired about sending his kids to the school, an offer was made that would allow him to coach a couple of teams in exchange for a discount on the monthly tuition. In that, a long relationship with Christ Community School was formed. He began to coach JV basketball and girls' softball. These choices were perfect considering his daughters were to be on the softball team and his son was interested in playing basketball. This arrangement gave him time with his kids while simultaneously allowing him the opportunity to minister and train on the ballfields and courts. It was an amazing outreach opportunity that did result in several teens visiting his church services from time to time. As his daughters were both in high school, the amount of teen boys visiting services rose exponentially. Rev. Englewilde called it "missionary dating", a term he used to describe the fact that boys were most likely attending for the girls and not solely for the Lord. Whatever the term, it was somewhat effective and a few of those teens accepted Christ as their Savior as a direct result of his family's presence on that school campus. Rev. Englewilde was occasionally asked to preach in the school's weekly chapel service. His style of preaching was quite different from what most students had ever heard. It was a nondenominational school, so the students came from varying religious backgrounds. They sat, wide-eyed and mesmerized, when Rev. Englewilde preached. He was exciting. He was dynamic. He moved around a lot! Some had never seen such in their own churches. He quickly became a favorite speaker throughout the school campus.

The fledgling little church continued to grow. There were a few key families in the community that had always been pillars and were influential in many community areas. The Kindred family was one. There was also the Landry family and the Lincoln family. The matriarch of the Landry family had been a florist in her younger days. She was well-known and loved throughout the community. In fact, it was her parents who had originally owned the land upon which the church sat and they had gifted it to the church decades prior. Her eldest son had been chief of police for ages and she had gained much respect throughout the community of Rosinton. Her younger son had helped hold the small church together while they had searched for a pastor. She was a saintly lady with a heart of gold. She never let anyone visit her home without giving them some gift, whether it was a trinket or a treat. The Lincolns were also instrumental in bringing Pastor Englewilde to Country Road Baptist Church. They had four grown children of their own, as well as a few grandchildren. Some came to church on occasion and others did not. They were burdened for the souls of their kids and grandkids. Not a service would go by that they didn't pray for their kids to be in church. Rev. Englewilde spent many hours visiting these and many others. He had a burden for the Rosinton community. The people held a special place in his heart. Partly, it was because this small handful of families had believed in him the first time, when he was only an 18-year-old kid, and had called him to pastor in their little community. The other part most likely stemmed from the fact that they, once again, believed in him in spite of the divorce. They were giving him the chance to pastor again and that meant more than anything to him. He had been called by God and that calling had been burning in his soul for four years. He knew it was what he was meant to do. Not being able to pastor had felt unnatural. He was more than ready to jump back in and do what God had called him to do. He was eager to pastor this flock, however small they may be.

Chapter 9

The Rosinton community within Baldwin County, Alabama quickly transitioned into a welcoming home for Rev. Englewilde and his children. They stayed with the Kindreds for a couple of months until their new mobile home could be set up on the property next to the church. A set-up was already in place on the property making it cost effective for the pastor to reside in close proximity to the church. Once again, he was on-call for the Lord and his congregants 24/7. He thoroughly enjoyed being in the ministry and pastoring again. He had a burden for Rosinton and beyond. He wanted to reach souls all over Baldwin County. The poor decisions of the previous minister along with a handful of other leaders in that location had left a sour taste in the mouths of those who lived within the community. He would have to endeavor tirelessly to rise above the stigma engrained within the minds of those in the community. Many had fallen out of church completely over incidents of the past. Many had vowed never to darken the doorway of the building again. The sign still reflected the old name, further associating the building and its congregants with past scandals. In March 1997, as Country Road Baptist Church began to grow under new leadership, the congregation decided, at the pastor's suggestion, to rename the church. Beacon Baptist Church would soon shed the stigma of the past and begin to flourish anew.

With a new name, a new coat of paint and updated pews were soon in the works. Slowly, they reached more and more families in the community. Saintly Mrs. Lincoln was thrilled to have several of her children and grandchildren begin to attend. She and her husband celebrated a milestone anniversary and hosted the festivities in the fellowship hall of the church. This occasion brought many different faces into the building, both new and old. The Lincolns were pillars in the small Rosinton community. People all over the county knew, loved, and respected the aging couple. Some of their friends had been in the building years prior when it had been under the old preacher and name. The excitement within the walls of the church enticed those friends of the Lincolns to visit services.

One young lady at the anniversary celebration by the name of Lydia caught the eye of Rev. Englewilde. He would later recall that she was the most beautiful woman he had ever seen. Her dark hair accented her crystal blue eyes. Her petite frame and mildly shy mannerisms only made her more attractive to him. He inquired of the Lincolns about this woman and her two-year-old son. They informed him that she, too, had once attended the church in those "old" days. In fact, she had been married to a lay preacher in the church, who had left her and their small son and had never looked back. He had abandoned the ministry and his family amidst the aforementioned scandals. For two years, she had raised her son alone while helping her sister and father care for her ailing mother around the clock. Her mother suffered from a debilitating condition and had long been bedridden and on ventilation. Lydia was the embodiment of meekness and her pale blue eyes shone when she smiled her sweet smile.

The Lincolns made introductions and arranged for a group to gather for ice cream following an evening service where Rev. Englewilde would have ample time to get to know her. The connection was instant. Her small son was smart as a whip and had an incredible sense of humor. He took a liking to the preacher. Having never had a father figure in his home, he instantly became the preacher's little buddy. The mother and son duo began to visit the church and to hang out afterwards with Rev. Englewilde and his kids. That little fella captured the hearts of the entire Englewilde family. His blue eyes shone bright with curiosity and his wild imagination was a constant source of entertainment. This tiny tot could tell the most elaborately long-winded stories. Lydia was quiet. Her son more than made up the conversations. As the preacher and Lydia spent more time together, they realized they shared similar goals and desires to live for the Lord. It did not take long for the preacher to realize she was more than special. On their second official date, he proposed marriage.

He made the engagement official during the Thanksgiving Celebration service at Beacon Baptist Church on a Wednesday night. They were surrounded by their children and the members of the church, the Lincolns included. It was no question in anyone's mind that this union would be a blessed one. The connection had been instant. Far beyond physical attraction, Rev. Englewilde saw in Lydia the qualities of a virtuous woman. She was kind and reserved. She was grace. She softened him. His defenses were unnecessary with her. There was a mutual trust, stemming from the need to rise above the past and cling to the hope of the future. There had been no logical, rational reason to put off the engagement nor was there a need to prolong it. They knew what God's will for their lives was and, with that assurance, they were left with only certainty. The date was set for the following February and the two families blended without missing a beat.

After their wedding there was a brief transition period within the home as the two teenage girls and their preteen brother adapted to having a new toddler brother. Angelisa and Trinity Reese took to the tike quite quickly. It was fun for them to have a new little brother. He was small and his bed matched his stature, so he was moved into the room with Angelisa since she was the oldest and, therefore, had the bigger room. Jacob, being the youngest and the only boy, already had the smallest room. This made it unlikely for the two boys to share a space, but Jacob enjoyed finally having another boy in the house to even things out. Angelisa loved hearing her new brother prattle away at night after the lights were off. His little mind had the imagination of a great storyteller. He would spin vivid tales, complete with sound effects to accompany any actions he was describing. The nearly three-year-old's blue eyes shone wild with excitement when he spoke. He blended into the family immediately, as did his mother. She was not the stereotypical stepmom. She was loving and never raised her voice. She had a level of patience rarely seen in a stepmother to teenagers. She stepped into a role that would scare the average woman and handled it all with grace and love. For the first time in years, Rev. Englewilde felt like he was emerging from the fog that had enveloped him and stepping back into the life for which he was created. He was, once again, pastoring. He was newly and happily married. He had his children with him and a new son as a bonus. He had a wonderful opportunity to minister while coaching at Christ Community School. Baldwin County held a special place in his heart. It would thereafter be synonymous with new beginnings.

Chapter 10

Life in Baldwin County became sweeter day by day. Rev. Englewilde settled into life with his new bride. The blended household buzzed with excitement. That excitement spilled out into their ministry. The girls continued to bring their teen friends to church services and youth outings, boosting the teen ministry. Jacob was playing on the JV basketball and baseball teams, giving him his own unique opportunity for outreach. The church grew in number and in spirit. With his new path clear and present, the preacher set about establishing a foundation in the Rosinton community. For the first time in what seemed like an eternity, he could see a long-term plan for his life. Lydia had been born and raised right there in the community and had never had a desire to leave. He felt like maybe this time God would allow him to settle in and put down permanent roots. For so long, his ministry had taken him from one fledgling community church to another, always seeming to move him on to the next ministry just as the current one seemed to be growing successfully. He had learned a lot since his last pastorate and he hoped to implement those lessons in his current position. He felt like he had a lot to prove. He wanted to prove to those watching that God's call is permanent. God had never revoked the calling he had placed on Warren Englewilde's life to preach the Gospel and pastor his flock. Many of his fellow pastor friends still would not have him in their pulpits to preach. At first, the divorce was the issue. Then it was the remarrying. This grieved his spirit. He loved to preach. He always had.

The calling on his life to preach the Gospel had come as a surprise to him, considering he had always suffered from crippling stage fright and was an introvert as a child and teen. But all of that dissipated when he was sharing the Gospel. The Holy Spirit took over him whenever he was in the pulpit and he was transformed into a mighty speaker with thunder and gumption. His second-grade speech therapist would have never believed that his tied-up tongue could preach so fast and so loud. The power he felt in the pulpit was unmatched in any other area of his life. His crippled foot didn't bother him when he was in the pulpit. There was an energy in his preaching that could only come from Heaven above. He usually suffered on Mondays, but, oh, how he loved to preach the Word of God! It excited him and animated him to tell others.

He also felt he had a lot to prove to himself. Underneath his tough exterior, he battled feelings of failure. His first marriage had ended. As hard as he had felt he had been trying, he had failed to hold it all together. The communication with his first wife had failed. Any attempt at resolution had failed. By failing to pay attention to the little issues at home, he had failed the ministry as well. He had felt out of control in the entire situation. Having spent a significant amount of time being separated from his children by such a great distance and then having to fight so desperately to regain them only fueled his resolve to hold everyone he loved near and dear. Now that he had Lydia and her young son as additions to his family, he had a new resolve to make changes. He felt he knew where he had failed before and vowed to himself to make the time for her and the children, even with the demands of a growing church ministry. He would not allow himself to fail again. He would be more attentive, more compassionate, and more understanding at home.

Lydia's young son had been named after his father, who had subsequently abandoned the two of them shortly after they were released from the hospital after his birth. He had been premature and was in the NICU for the first few months of his tiny life. He had beaten the odds against him and grew to be a little fighter. He was nicknamed Spunky and it stuck, considering no one wanted to call him by his given name which only reminded them of the man who had run off. He lived up to that nickname too. He had more spunk than anyone the preacher had ever met.

Not eight weeks after their wedding, the Englewilde newlyweds got some quite unexpected news. Lydia was pregnant; they were blessed with a honeymoon baby. The excitement within the walls of their household tripled as the blended bunch rallied to make plans for the new arrival. The children were once again shifted around to different bedrooms to accommodate the additional child. The girls, who had only recently been permitted to split up and have their own rooms for the first time in their lives, were once again placed in the largest of the bedrooms. Spunky and Jacob would room together and the smallest room would be converted into a nursery since it was the closest in proximity to the parents' room.

The months whizzed by as the older kids busied themselves with school and extracurricular activities. Rev. Englewilde continued to coach a few teams at Christ Community School and Spunky tagged along as his trusty assistant.

Lydia had struggled with her first pregnancy so she was cautious this time around, careful to follow the doctor's instructions and fearful that she may wind up with another premature baby. An ultrasound revealed that this baby was to be another boy. This was a great relief to the preacher. He had his hands full with the two teenage daughters he had. Not that they were really any trouble, but the constant threat of teenage hormones was enough to cause any father to lose sleep. He was approaching forty and swore his heart couldn't stand to raise another girl at his age.

Lydia only suffered a couple small complications and was able to carry little Daniel to full term. He was born the day after her twenty-seventh birthday. He had a head full of dark, wild hair that stood straight up as if he had been frightened. They all swore it was because Trinity Reese had loved to scream silly things at Lydia's pregnant belly. The house was full of random, ridiculous giggles. The age range between the preacher's first three kids and the other boys was broad but they always seemed to get along with each other. They formed a strong family bond. Angelisa loved to take her little brothers with her when she drove around town. She had only recently received her license when Daniel was born so she looked for any excuse to drive to the grocery store for Lydia or her dad. She and Trinity Reese had never spent much time around babies but they quickly bonded with baby Daniel, even allowing him to sleep in a bassinet in their room.

Lydia appreciated the extra help that the two teenage girls provided. She found that recovering from her second pregnancy was much easier than the first. She was surrounded by her new family and had a support system she had never before had. Her own mother had been ill and on life support throughout both of her pregnancies. She could not rely on her parents for help when her first husband had left. She had grown accustomed to being alone. Now she and Spunky had a new life with the preacher and she had acquired three half-grown kids. Sure, the house was much louder now and life held a few more chaotic qualities, but the house was a happy one. It was filled to the brim with love and laughter.

Rev. Englewilde was not completely satisfied. His church was growing. His family was growing. His ministry was growing. But he wanted more. He began a prison ministry with one of the couples in the church. He would preach and Bro. Trout would provide music. Bro. Trout had been a successful singer in nightclubs before he had given his life to the Lord. He then began to use his talents on Sundays for the Lord rather than on Saturdays for the world. Brother and Mrs. Trout took over the organization of the prison ministry. They would schedule and plan meetings within the prison systems in Alabama, Louisiana, Mississippi, Florida, and Georgia. They were a small team but were quickly doing a mighty work. Their travels took them across many miles and hundreds of inmates heard the Gospel behind the prison walls. Many hardened criminals – both men and women - accepted the Gospel presented to them and their lives were forever changed because of the burden this team of three had for their souls. Rev. Englewilde rejoiced with each new addition into the family of God. How mighty He was to reach down and save those with whom society had cut ties! Seeing grown men weep as they fell to their knees and accepted Christ as their Savior was the sweetest sight to the preacher.

To him, there was nothing better than reaching those who were seemingly hopeless.

Between the prison ministry, the growing church, and his growing family, the preacher was as busy as he had ever been. He recruited a few men in the church to go to training classes so they could help the prison ministry out. They were able to form teams of two or three to go and rotated those teams out to give the preacher a chance to catch his breath. What this led to was the addition of more prison meetings on the schedule. Rev. Englewilde struck up a friendly relationship with local law officers and the warden at the nearest correctional facility. He was able to arrange a bus transport each Sunday to bring inmates to morning services. The inmates were to sign up with the warden each week if they wished to attend. If they maintained good behavior throughout the week, they were granted permission to take the transport bus to Beacon Baptist for regular Sunday morning worship. While at first, some of the members were a little reserved about the idea, they quickly got to know the men and also began to share their pastor's burden. For some, the circumstances that led to incarceration were the result of bad decision making. For others, the prisoners were born into situations in which crime was a way of life. They all had one thing in common. They needed the Lord. It is the one universal factor for all of humanity.

The preacher was pleased with all of the new developing ministries. He and his congregation were reaching souls for Christ. They had begun to focus on their own communities within Baldwin County individually. Collectively, they supported missionaries all over the globe, one of which was Rev. Englewilde's dear friend Paul Amon and his wife Anna. They had surrendered to be missionaries abroad and had raised their three children in the Philippines, preaching and teaching the Gospel. The pastor had always held a special place for Paul. The Lord blessed the congregation of Beacon Baptist to be able to regularly give to the families around the globe who had given up the luxuries of their American comforts to live in a foreign land to declare the Gospel. Rev. Englewilde shared his burden for missions with the members of church and they were able to fully see the reach they could have for the Lord if they gave out of the abundance of their hearts. He began to take a weekly penny offering on Wednesday nights before the children were dismissed to the Patch the Pirate Club lessons. The penny, he would say, represents one cent. A missionary is also one sent. The congregation was encouraged to pick up any pennies they may see lying around throughout the week and pray for a missionary. Then they could bring those pennies in on Wednesday evenings for the penny offering, when children went around gathering the loose change from the older members of the congregation and brought them forward. They were thrown into an old Kentwood water cooler jug and collected until it was too heavy to lift. Then the change would be counted, sorted, and sent to a missionary with a special need. The children, as well as the adults, all learned that the smallest offering can be used to make a very large impact. The members of Beacon Baptist Church in Rosinton, Alabama were alive with excitement and on fire for God. They were ready and willing to reach the world with the Gospel. Rev. Englewilde was on cloud nine as he led this flock with his family at his side.

Chapter 11

Beacon Baptist Church and all of its ministries flourished as Rev. Englewilde and his family worked tirelessly in the Rosinton Community. The prison outreach was seeing souls saved on a weekly basis. They had been consistently adding new missionaries each year to support. By the end of the year 2000, Rev. Englewilde was preparing to marry off his oldest daughter Angelisa. She had graduated high school earlier that spring. She had always had one goal in life: to be a good wife and mother someday. College had never really been in her plans, even though her grades were impeccable. She had met a young man out in Texas while visiting her mom. She and Easton had dated for a while in the summer between her junior and senior years, spent a few months apart because of the difficulty of long-distance relationships, then realized neither wanted to be apart from the other ever again. He proposed to her in August and they planned a wedding to be held at Beacon Baptist in mid-December. The wedding preparations, along with the usual hustle and bustle of the season, added an extra level of pressure on the entire Englewilde family. The community was a huge blessing. One of the teachers from Christ Community School offered to make the wedding cake as a gift because of their long-standing friendship with "Coach" Englewilde. A lady from the congregation of the church offered to cater the reception. Angelisa and Trinity Reese purchased silk flowers and made the arrangements and decorations themselves, with help from their mother and Lydia. Everyone rallied to make the wedding happen with as little chaos as possible before the holidays.

The newlyweds were also gifted a honeymoon trip to the mountains. It was tough for the preacher to say goodbye to his daughter, even though she and her new husband would reside only a few miles away and in the Rosinton community. Not only had his ministry branched out, but it seemed his family was now branching out as well. It was difficult to believe she had grown already - eighteen and married. She was no longer a child, although she would always and forever remain his little girl. They had always shared a bond. The household would feel strange without her living there anymore.

After all the excitement of the wedding and the holidays died back down, the preacher settled in to his various ministry opportunities. His basketball team at the school was on fire. They had won several games during the season and were headed to a championship tournament. The church had begun a weekly visitation program, which provided the congregation a chance to visit the shut-ins and elderly of the community who could not physically attend services. This also provided an opportunity of outreach to greet those within the community who may be looking for a church home. Beacon Baptist Church really began to shine throughout the Rosinton community. When the new nursing home facility opened up down the road, Rev. Englewilde was able to set up a weekly Sunday service in their multipurpose room. They would take a team of people each Sunday afternoon who would visit the patient's rooms and give assistance to those who wished to join them for the service. So many of those elderly faces lit up when the old hymns were sung! Even those who had long forgotten their loved ones, gripped with the curse of dementia, seemed to recall those old hymns. They enjoyed the preacher's old-fashioned, dynamic preaching style. He reminded them of the church services of their youth. The family members who regularly visited the patients within the walls of the nursing home noticed an excitement in the demeanor of their aged loved ones and began to attend the services as well. The seeds that Rev. Englewilde had begun to plant when he first arrived in Baldwin County had taken root, and those roots had branched out to form an outreach network of which he could have never dreamed alone. God was certainly working through him and his congregation at Beacon Baptist.

In the fall of 2001, Angelisa gave birth to the preacher's first grandchild. Rev. Englewilde paced with impatience in the waiting room, anxiously awaiting the birth. It was Wednesday afternoon and Angelisa had been in labor all day long. He had not arranged for anyone to take his place in the pulpit for that night's midweek service.

He did not typically miss a church service- not for any reason. The minutes ticked by as the other family members took their turns going in and visiting with Angelisa. The preacher, when his turn came to go back, checked on her to see how she was and reminded her that he would need to leave by 5:30 p.m. in order to prepare for the evening's service. She laughed, assuring him that she was doing her best and she understood if he needed to leave before the actual birth. He returned to the waiting room where Lydia and his parents and the other children waited, along with Angelisa's mom, stepdad and maternal grandparents. It was quite a full room. Summer Louise was born at 5:18 p.m. in just enough time for the preacher to catch a glimpse of her tiny little six-pound eight-ounce body, complete with ten tiny toes and ten tiny fingers, before he left the hospital. Ever the dutiful daughter, Angelisa had somehow managed to give birth right on time. Rev. Englewilde beamed with pride as he told the congregation all about his perfect little granddaughter, with her blue eyes and turned up nose.

Rev. Englewilde had always had a knack for coming up with neat ideas to get his congregation excited about serving the Lord. The penny offering would go on to be an established trait of the church. Another of his most remembered ideas occurred on a big attendance day for the church. In 2002, Rev. Englewilde organized a God and

Country Day to commemorate the first anniversary of the September 11 attack on America. After the birth of his granddaughter, Angelisa had come to work as his secretary on a part-time basis to allow her the freedom of bringing young Summer with her to work. He had needed the help for some time and she needed a little extra cash. Angelisa helped him to compile a list of names and agencies within Baldwin County. He and the members of Beacon Baptist Church wanted to honor all those who publicly served and protected their community. The preacher had always had a deep patriotic love for America. He had a quite extensive collection of American bald eagle figurines. Some, he had purchased for himself, but most had been gifts from various people he had ministered to over the course of his adult lifetime. Even his most requested sermon was strongly based on the life of the eagle and the symmetry of that life with the life of a Christian. The church rallied and promoted their big day ahead of time. They contacted the local newspapers and made sure a sizable ad was printed in the Community Events section. They visited each and every police station, fire station, EMS station, and sheriff's office in the county to hand deliver an invitation for all available to attend. The ladies of the church met and planned a delicious meal to serve all of their honored guests after the service. It would consist of fried chicken, potato salad, baked beans, and homemade buttermilk biscuits - a perfect southern lunch!

On the big day, many uniformed public servants from varying community agencies were in attendance. There was an excitement in the air. American flags lined the roadway out in front of the church. Additional parking was provided by the owners of the land adjacent to the church. Patriotic décor lined the walls of the sanctuary, foyer, and hallways inside. When Pastor Englewilde stepped out of his office, dressed from head to toe like Uncle Sam, all eyes were on him. His star-spangled top hat glistened in the morning sun and complimented the striped suit that accompanied it. He greeted each visitor with a warm, welcoming handshake and enjoyed the chuckles of delight from members and visitors alike. As the service began, he greeted the congregation and noticed that even the local news media had slipped in at the back of the building. One by one, he had each agency representative present stand and introduce themselves. There wasn't a dry eye in the overcrowded auditorium as these men and women were recognized and applauded. The preacher stood, looking out over the congregation filled with community leaders, police officers, county deputies, paramedics, firemen, and local politicians – a sea of people from right there in the Rosinton community - whose lives were dedicated to serving and protecting the same community for which he had a burden. He was humbled that they would take their time to come and allow him and his congregation the chance to say "thank you". He was honored anew to be a part of such a wonderful community of people. Feeling doubly blessed, he took the pulpit and gave each and every one in attendance the best gift he could ever offer - the Gospel of Christ.

The preacher was on a spiritual high. The many outreach ministries he had begun were taking off and reaching people all across Baldwin County. He and his family were busy working to reach everyone they could reach for the Lord. Aside from their ministry duties, there was also school and sports for the kids and work for Lydia. She had begun to work in the daycare down the road to help supplement the household's income. Feeding four growing, active kids required more than just the weekly salary of a country preacher. They got a rare few days break from their schedules and took a couple of hours drive north to visit the preacher's little brother Dan. Dan was in the paper business and had worked his way up to be quite successful in the industry. He had a home set in the country a little north of the Mobile river delta. It was a sportsman's dream. All three of the Englewilde boys had been raised hunting and fishing. The preacher didn't get many opportunities to do either and he jumped at any chance he could to go up and visit Dan and his wife Clara. Their two children Noah and Beth were the same ages as Angelisa and Trinity Reese. Jacob, being a few years younger than Noah, had always sort of idolized his older cousin. To be honest, all of the cousins did. He was never one to act like he was too cool to have fun. On the contrary, he was always the one to make everyone laugh. He and Beth loved the country lifestyle they had. They were active in FFA and raised show steers and dairy cows throughout their adolescence. Spunky and Daniel also loved going to visit. Their Uncle Dan would often play jokes on them and wrestle with them in the yard.

The preacher took his old pickup truck on the trip. It had been acting up and he wanted Dan to take a look at it while they were visiting. Trinity Reese, Spunky, Daniel, and Jacob all piled out of the cab and ran excitedly to greet their cousins, aunt, and uncle in the driveway. They had plenty of land to run and play and explore at Uncle Dan's house. Noah, Jacob, and little Daniel quickly planned an afternoon hunting trip. Daniel loved to go hunting with his big brother and cousin. He couldn't wait to be bigger so he could trade his BB gun in for a rifle or a shotgun. They all disappeared into the woods and wouldn't be back until dark.

The men took the opportunity to attend to the truck while the ladies visited and Beth and Trinity Reese did whatever it is that teenage girls do. They put the truck up on ramps and determined there was an issue with the transmission. After diagnosing the issue, they took a quick ride to the nearest auto parts store for the required replacement parts and then were back at work in no time. With the hood up, Dan worked from the topside while Warren slid underneath to work from the bottom side. Just as they disconnected the transmission from the truck, it began to roll! There was no stopping it! It all happened so fast but it felt like slow motion as Dan watched in horror while the truck slowly came to a stop again - on top of his older brother! Warren Englewilde was pinned under the weight of a '91 Ford F150 and Dan quickly scrambled for help. He called out to the boys across the field. He hoped they could hear him from where they had chosen to hunt. He yelled for Clara to call 911. All the while, the preacher's chest was pinned under the massive load. He tried not to panic, but that proved to be impossible. They were far out in the country, miles from the nearest medical facility and almost two hours away from a real hospital. He knew it would take many long grueling minutes before any help at all could arrive. He tried to move, just a little, but the pain was excruciating. It was a struggle for him to just breathe, let alone cry out in pain. The full weight of the truck was pinning his torso to the ground and there was no way his brother and the others could push it back up the ramps without assistance. So, he waited. Dan, Clara, and Lydia clamored to try to help. Lydia kept calling out to him, making him reply to be sure he was ok. They were afraid the weight of the truck may collapse his lungs or even crush his ribs. It seemed like an eternity before they heard the faint sirens off in the distance. Slowly, they drew closer until their ear-piercing alarms were seemingly right next to the preacher's feet, which were still visible under the front bumper of the pickup. He heard the rush of emergency responders and volunteer firefighters scrambling to gain knowledge of what was going on, then, all at once, they rallied and pushed the truck, relieving the massive pressure from his chest and sliding him out from under the truck with as much care as possible. He had thought that the removal of the truck from his torso would be a relief, but a new wave of pain washed over him. The blood was rushing to all the places that hurt, and that seemed to be every part of his upper body. Agony gripped his entire upper body. Instinctively he flinched and tried to wrap his arms around his chest to hold in the pain. This instinct just caused him more pain. His arms ached. His chest throbbed. Breathing sent dagger-like shooting pains all throughout his lungs. He wanted to scream but that would have just been an agonizing torture to inflict upon himself. They placed him on a gurney with a panicked Lydia following close beside him. She quickly called Angelisa to inform her of what had happened. All the boys had come back from their hunting expedition in the woods and Trinity Reese and Beth had been crying and watching the chaos from the front porch. Everyone was in fearful anticipation, waiting to hear what the damage to the preacher would be. He was transported to the closest medical facility for examination, x-rays, and treatment. That facility was actually a nursing home which had a community clinic in one of its wings. It was less than ideal for an emergency situation such as this but it would have to do for the time being. A prayer chain was quickly forming as Angelisa, back home, scrambled to call everyone she could. All they could do now was pray and wait for test and image results to come back.

Chapter 12

X-rays showed that several of the preacher's ribs were severely bruised and two of them were fractured. He was released from the little clinic and sent home to follow up with his own doctor. The medications he was given only numbed his senses but not his pain. The long ride home was quite uncomfortable, made only slightly better by the fact he would not be returning home in the broken-down old pick-up, which still sat in his brother's yard waiting to be pieced back together. Recovery would be painful, but the injuries were not nearly as bad as many had feared they would be. It had been a real scare. 2002 had started out on a rough foot. The first few months were excruciating and the pain in his ribs affected every aspect of his life. Rev. Englewilde was a talker - an expressive talker at that. To have difficulty drawing a breath and expressing himself was one thing, but to add to it the soreness of his arms and chest made communication near impossible for the usually animated and verbose preacher.

He was able to slowly recover and regain mobility in time to see Trinity Reese off to college in the Fall of 2002. She had dreamed for years of the chance to go to LSU, a dream that was born during their brief time in Louisiana. She had been accepted and received enough financial aid to cover the costs of her tuition, room, and books. Tiger pride was flowing freely as the entire family gathered for a farewell party in her honor. Angelisa and Lydia had planned and cooked snacks for the gathering, with Summer toddling underfoot and sampling all the goodies. All of Trinity Reese's friends from school had been invited, as well as the teens from the youth group and several families from the church who had been friends and mentors to her throughout her high school years. To be sending her to a university was a delight and honor for everyone who had had a part in influencing her and teaching her. Rev. Englewilde swelled with pride as he watched his second born daughter flit around the gathering, greeting and laughing and enjoying her last afternoon at home. It seemed his family was steadily branching out now.

In the winter of 2002, Angelisa announced that his second grandchild was to arrive the following July. The whole family was buzzing with excitement. Trinity Reese was enrolled in a competitive nursing program at LSU. The boys were all doing well in school and sports. The preacher had all but recovered from the truck incident. The church was thriving in its many ministries and all seemed to be in peaceful harmony. The Englewilde men had a long-standing tradition to take their boys to the river swamp every November. The trip was an incredible time for them to bond while enjoying nature and teaching their boys to hunt and fish. The weather was its usual warm 65, even in the late days of November, but the water in the Mobile River Delta was cold and swift. Rev. Englewilde and Jacob, his two brothers Rusty and Dan, their boys Noah and Presley, along with their patriarch Grandad Forrest all gathered and launched their small fleet of boats in the mid-day Alabama heat. The layers of camo they had packed seemed frivolous under the southern sun, but they knew from experience the nights could bring a chill. They set out upriver to find the best island to make camp. After about an hour and a half of boating upriver, they approached a small cluster of islands that rarely were hunted. They had scouted these out in the weeks prior to their trip and knew that no one seemed to frequent that particular location and figured they'd have their best chance to have a successful hunt in that location. The islands were close enough that the small 10 ft. John boat they had brought along could be used to hop between land masses easily, even for the younger boys.

Noah was almost 21, so he took up the lead with Jacob, 16, and Presley, 15. They pitched their tents and gathered kindling for the night's fire, then Noah and Jacob set out in the little boat to see if they could get lucky finding a deer before supper. The men stayed back along with Presley to ready the rest of the camp before nightfall. They had begun their hunt in the wee hours of the morning and were exhausted from the day's travel. Knowing that Noah and Jacob would be back by supper, the men settled in and enjoying talking and catching up with one another. The family had always been close and they shared their problems and victories with one another. They also joked and laughed, having a good time just being together away from the noise of work and everyday issues.

As they laughed and shared old memories from the past, they realized that time had gotten away from them. It had grown dark and was past time for them to start supper. It was also past time for Noah and Jacob to return. They figured the boys may have come up on a deer, but no shots had been heard yet. They readied their supper and waited. Time ticked on and still no word from the boys.

Meanwhile, Noah and Jacob had come across a slough in between two of the little islands and had chosen to take the little boat up into the tiny waterway. They thought it looked like a spot uninhabited by previous hunters. They were probably right, considering the slough was extremely narrow and full of fallen logs and river debris. It had grown dark while they were scouting around in there and they knew their fathers and grandfather would begin to worry. As they maneuvered the little boat in the darkness back through the swift current, they hit a log that was hidden under the surface of the water. The boat hit the log just right to send the boys overboard in the deep, littered, icy water. Noah got caught in the current and was pinned under a log, barely able to keep his face above water as his layers of camo became waterlogged and pulled him down deeper into the water. The current pushed his body into the logs with full force. He scrambled to get a hold of something to help him out of the water, but was unsuccessful. Jacob was clamoring and sputtering water on the other side of the boat, barely maintaining control of it to keep it from washing away and leaving them stranded. It took him a minute or two to register in the darkness that his cousin was in real trouble. He managed to get the boat pulled up on the bank and jumped back in to help Noah. Hard as he tried, he was unable to get Noah out of the tangle of logs. His boot was caught in the web of branches under the water and only his face was above water as the current rushed and rippled around him. The tide was rising. Holding his head up was becoming impossible. Jacob pulled and tugged on him with all his might, but Noah was older and significantly stockier than Jacob. His efforts were only burning his energy at a rapid pace. He quickly scrambled back out of the water, crawled over to the boat, and fired off his rifle. He knew if the dads heard a shot this long after dark that they'd take notice. At first, they would be mad at the boys for hunting after dark. Knowing this, and knowing there wasn't time to waste. Jacob fired off two more shots. He hoped this would not only get the attention of the men back at camp but also would give them an idea of their location. It was dark and the excitement of fighting for his life and now his cousin's life had him completely turned around.

After firing the rifle a few times, he hopped back in the water to assist the struggling Noah, who was growing extremely fatigued from the constant fight against the current. Jacob held him around the chest and kept his face above water. They tried not to panic as the moment slowly ticked by, hoping the men had heard their distress call.

At last, they heard a faint voice calling in the distance. They frantically yelled for help. Within moments, there was splashing in the water near them accompanied by the beams of flashlights. Other hunters in the area had heard their shots and come quickly to assist. The men jumped into the water and worked quickly to free Noah from the logs and debris and to drag him up on the bank of the river. Exhausted from the struggle, Noah relaxed, seemingly lifeless, the strangers along with Jacob frantically surrounded him, not knowing if he needed space or resuscitation. He coughed and heaved, alerting them that he was breathing, if not easily, and would probably be ok if they could get him warmed up. Having had a few minutes to collect his thoughts and regain his senses, Jacob remember which direction his dad and the others were camping and told the strangers if they would help Noah into the boat, he could get him back to camp to dry off and warm up.

When the boys arrived back at the family campsite, the men had definitely begun to worry and had sent Dan out to search while the others stayed close and quiet, hoping to hear them rustling around on their return. They still held hope that the boys were merely late because they have found a deer. They held hope that neither had been injured. When they small boat came into view, they saw that it was accompanied by another boat. The strangers got out and helped Jacob drag the boat ashore and helped Noah ease out of it and onto the sandy bank. He shivered uncontrollably in his drenched camo. The strangers greeted the group of puzzled faces surrounding the campfire and recounted the events as they had understood them. Dan arrived back at the campsite to see his shivering son limply lying near the fire, struggling to regain energy after the long fight with the logs and the current.

Noah was winded and extremely fatigued, but he was otherwise unharmed. The strangers ventured back through the darkness to their own camp upriver and the Englewilde men all gathered around Noah and praised God that he was safe. They also helped him out of his wet clothes to better help him warm next to the fire. Jacob, too, was shaking uncontrollably. His drenched clothes and the adrenaline of the whole ordeal had sent his body into convulsions. They sat next to each other by the fire and breathed a unified sigh of relief as they realized how close they'd both come to losing their lives in the rushing, rising current. God had put those strangers nearby for a purpose. They had thought their family was all alone in the river swamp. God had those men just close enough to hear their shots of distress. They had come to the boys' aid at just the right moment. Any later would have resulted in tragedy. They boys knew this as they stared at the flames of the fire and breathed an internal prayer of thanks. They would remember His faithfulness that night for the rest of their lives.

Chapter 13

The year 2002 had turned out to be one of many exciting and trying experiences for Rev. Englewilde and his family. Even his church had shared in some of that intensity of emotion. Their prayer chain had worked overtime and everyone was ready for a fresh start as 2003 dawned. The previous year had included some scary situations that had turned out with much better outcomes than what they could have resulted in. The recovery from the truck had been trying physically. The boys' run-in up the river had been physically draining for them and it had been emotionally taxing on the entire family as they reflected on what could have been. They hoped the New Year would bring happier circumstances. Their hopes would soon fail them, for the Englewilde family was to experience a great deal of heartache before they would rejoice again.

A series of sad events began to occur in the lives of the Englewilde's, beginning with Lydia experiencing a miscarriage very early into her third pregnancy. Little Daniel had just turned four the previous November, making the timing for a new baby perfect. They were still in the happy stages of rejoicing over the news when she lost the baby. Not only were the expectant parents deeply saddened, but so were the siblings, who were mostly grown by this point. With Angelisa being pregnant with her second daughter, Rev. Englewilde and Lydia had looked forward to sharing that experience with their daughter in a very unique way. Trinity Reese was off at college, successfully mastering her tough nursing classes and working part-time to pay for living expenses. Jacob was wrapping up his junior year in high school and looking ahead to future possibilities. Hearing the news on the heels of discovering the pregnancy had disheartened the whole lot of them.

They wiped their tears and tried to make sense of the loss. The loss of young lives is always toughest to reconcile in our minds. To lose a child you've never had the chance to meet is a devastating blow. To lose one you've had years to get to know is soul-crushing.

The call came early. It was a Saturday morning, too early for the sun just yet. Warren Englewilde answered the phone that rang just next to him in his living room recliner. He knew it must be an important issue, just by looking at the clock on the wall. He had it before it had fully rung its first ring. The voice on the other end was broken and unfamiliar. It took him a moment to recognize his little brother Dan. Such despair was in his voice. Warren straightened up in the chair and implored Dan to take it easy and tell him what was going on. "It's Noah" is all he could sob through the broken gasps of sorrow. Another voice came on the line. A neighbor had taken the phone from Dan to convey the news to Warren. Noah had been driving to work in the wee hours of the morning. He had been hit by a drunk driver. He never even knew what hit him. The EMS workers on scene said they didn't believe he had felt a thing, as he had died on impact. It was soul-crushing devastation. Warren hung up immediately and called Jacob down the hall. Jacob sleepily stepped into the living room to see his father weeping in his chair. Warren conveyed to Jacob the news he had just received and the two sat, embraced and silent, for a few moments. Warren readied himself to drive up to his brother's place to offer assistance and comfort. Jacob was sent to tell his very pregnant sister the tragic news.

When she heard a knock at her door a little after 6 a.m. on a Saturday, Angelisa didn't know who it could be. She had just fixed herself a cup of coffee and settled into her couch to enjoy it. She only had two weeks left before her little one was due to be born and she relished the quiet moments of the morning before little Summer woke for the day. When she opened the door to see Jacob, she was momentarily speechless. She knew by the look on his face and the hour of the weekend morning that it was not just a friendly visit. When he told her to sit down, all of the blood drained from her body and she went cold. She knew it wasn't going to be good news at all. As he told her that Noah had been in accident, she lost all composure. He had been her favorite cousin. He'd been everyone's favorite. It didn't feel real. She felt like she was floating overhead, watching this all unfold but not believing it. Jacob tried to be strong for his big sister. But Angelisa knew that he had looked up to Noah just as much, if not more, than she had. They had bonded that past year, especially after the incident up the river. It pained her to know he felt he had to hold his own feelings back on her account.

As she struggled against herself to regain her composure, her mind was whirring with thoughts. When had she last spoken to Noah? They had had plans to get together soon, but *soon* would never come now. None of what her brother had just told her made any sense at all. Her head spun with the news. She implored of him what she should do. Should she drive up to be with her Uncle Dan and Aunt Clara? And her cousin Beth, who had just lost her only sibling - how was she coping? What could possibly be done to make this tragic situation any easier? She was reeling with emotion and the urge to do *something*. Jacob assured her that there was nothing at the present moment that she could do but to take care of herself. He didn't want her to get all worked up and cause trauma to her unborn baby. As he left her front door and closed it behind him, she collapsed to the floor and sobbed a prayer to God to hold dear the bleeding hearts that were affected by the tragedy. Her heart was broken and she stayed crumpled in the floor, praying, until the tears would no longer fall.

Rev. Englewilde stayed by Dan's side throughout the entire funeral planning process. Rusty, too, had come up to help with his daughter Layla, who was just a couple months older than Noah. Everyone was taking the sudden loss extremely hard. On the day of the funeral, Lydia and Angelisa rode together with the other siblings to meet their grieving family at the funeral home. Forrest and his wife Marie, the figurative heads of the Englewilde family, struggled to maintain a brave face for their boys and their families. Losing Noah had dealt a devastating blow to their entire extended family. He was loved throughout his community and beyond and there were people arriving in droves to pay their respects – including the boy who had been behind the wheel that fateful morning and taken Noah's life with his careless actions. The family all had differing reactions to his being there. Some were offended that he would show his face. Others were comforted by his bravery and sincerity of spirit. The Gospel of Christ was preached in the service, sharing the hope that is found in Jesus. This hope had been accepted by Noah and the family rejoiced through their sadness at the knowledge that they would one day be reunited with the son/grandson/brother/cousin they loved so much.

Lydia had been hurting in her back the entire morning. She thought that maybe she had merely slept in an odd position, but, as the day plodded on, the pain intensified and became unbearable. As the family wrapped up the graveside service and ventured back to the church for a meal that had been provided for them by the people of their church and community, Warren and Lydia excused themselves and headed straight for the hospital to have her checked out. The emergency room was somewhat empty, considering it was a mid-day and midweek. They had called ahead to her doctor to be sure this was an issue for the emergency room rather than an office visit. Tests were run on Lydia and two very definite results came back: she would need emergency gallbladder surgery and she was pregnant. The first revelation was scary and unexpected, but the second revelation was even scarier and even more unexpected. It was determined that she must have gotten pregnant not long after suffering the miscarriage weeks prior. Being pregnant would make the gallbladder surgery slightly more tedious, but manageable. The surgeon seemed confident that he could take care of the issue with no risk to the very young unborn child Lydia was carrying. She was immediately prepped for the procedure and whisked away to the operating room. Rev. Englewilde paced in the waiting room, reluctant to call his grieving family to notify them of what was going on. He was alone. There had been many times throughout his life in which he had felt the despair of loneliness, but this instance felt more isolated than any of the rest. This woman, whom he loved and cherished so much, was lying in the operating room and also was expecting his child. He was scared. He wept as he prayed to God to have His healing hand of mercy on his precious wife. God had blessed him immensely when he had brought Lydia into his life. She had healed a part of him that had been broken. He didn't mind suffering himself but it grieved him to know his wife was in any pain at all.

When the surgeon came out to assure him that all had gone according to plan, he was beyond relieved. Only then did he allow himself to contact his parents, brothers, and children about the day's occurrences. Lydia was through the worst of it and he had not wished to cause any of his grieving loved ones more reason to worry. Within the hour, several of those he contacted came walking through the door, admonishing him for taking so long to inform them. No one should go through such fiery trials alone. They rejoiced with him that she would be ok and his daughters shrieked with excitement when they heard the news of the pregnancy. They needed to hear the joyous news on such an otherwise somber day. Their family had suffered a great deal of sorrow over the preceding days and they needed any shred of hope to cling to in order to begin the healing process that always follows the loss of someone dear. While nothing could ever make up for the loss, it was nice to have a reason to rise up and look forward to the future. One life had been tragically taken from them. Now, there would soon be a new life within the Englewilde family - new life and new hope.

Chapter 14

As Angelisa neared her due date, she and Lydia enjoyed going to appointments together in anticipation of both of their new little ones' arrivals. Angelisa gave birth to a healthy baby girl in July 2003 and Lydia gave birth to an adorable bouncing boy the following February. The new additions provided much needed joy to Warren and his family. The preacher was, once again, a proud new father to baby Winston while simultaneously rejoicing over a new granddaughter, Autumn. He felt his new son would keep him young a little bit longer, even if Angelisa insisted on continuing to make him a grandfather time and time again. As one son was born, another was preparing to graduate high school. Jacob had been offered many opportunities. Being a skilled basketball player and having broken several records at Christ Community School, he had several options for college. He had worked and apprenticed under some very skilled carpenters and craftsmen all throughout his high school years. This had given him a well-rooted knowledge of the trade and he had real passion for it. He and Lily Kindred had begun to date and her feelings from childhood had grown from a puppy-love crush to much more. He had begun to feel those same feelings for her and he wasn't sure if he wanted to give that up. He had many alternate paths laid ahead him. The preacher and Jacob prayed daily for God's direction in his life.

In the end, Jacob opted to go to community college nearby so he could play ball and earn a degree while working part-time to continue to fine-tune his woodworking and carpentry talents. He helped renovate several rooms at Beacon Baptist Church, which gained the attention of some prominent members of the community with his natural talent and fine craftsmanship.

With just the three young boys Spunky, Daniel, and Winston at home now and his older three having branched out and begun their lives, Lydia and Warren settled into a more active daily routine. She was still working at a local childcare facility while he juggled pastoring and coaching at Christ Community School. The prison ministry was thriving and growing so rapidly that they formed three different prison teams to do weekly services in facilities, in Alabama and surrounding states. Souls were coming to know the love, grace, and mercy of Jesus Christ on a weekly basis. Lives were being changed and the blessing of their labor was being manifested ten-fold at Beacon Baptist Church. Not only was the prison ministry growing, but the youth ministry was also growing. Rev. Englewilde had hired his friend, Liam, from Louisiana to come in and lead the youth ministries. He had met Liam when he had worked and lived in Louisiana. Then, Liam had been one of the young adults that would frequently come over to watch TV and eat pizza on the weekends. He had quickly become like an older brother to Angelisa, Trinity Reese, and Jacob. Having him join the staff at Beacon Baptist Church was nothing but God-inspired. Liam was relatable to youth of all ages and had a way of teaching and preaching that really got their attention. Part of it was definitely the fact that he enjoyed kicking trash cans while he taught the youth class. It was effective at gaining their attention. He took over the van ministry and regularly filled it to over-capacity. He knew his Bible and he knew how to keep the teens and preteens engaged in the Word of God. An excitement filled the walls of Beacon Baptist Church and it reverberated throughout the community until the biggest problem the church had was a lack of parking. God was working big time in Baldwin County and Rev. Englewilde's heart soared as he saw all the new faces coming to experience what God was doing. They enjoyed a very successful couple of years without incident or accident.

In 2006, the Lord impressed upon the preacher's heart to start a different type of outreach ministry for the community. He had a burden to provide affordable, quality childcare with a Christian emphasis. Lydia had worked for various childcare centers around the county and had been trained and certified by the health department. She was taking their youngest son Winston to work with her, but they still charged her a fee to bring him, even though he was in her room and in her care all day. It did not make sense to be paying the daycare to watch him if it was, in fact, his own mother watching over him. The leaders of the church met and voted to do the necessary upgrades in order to open their own church-based daycare.

Jacob was hired to do the contract work for the renovations to the church nursery, which would act as daycare center throughout the week and remain the nursery during regular church services. Angelisa worked evenings to provide an artful array of wall décor to transform the room into a scene from Noah's Ark. She was diligently working her duties as church secretary during the daytime hours by taking out advertisements for the upcoming new daycare in all of the local papers. An official start date was announced for mid-February and Beacon Baptist Daycare opened its doors with its first full-time applicants - Summer, Autumn, and Winston.

Before the week was out, they had applications from a dozen new families, all seeking an affordable and safe environment to entrust with their children while they worked. It was a learning process for both Lydia, as she ran the day-to-day responsibilities, and for the preacher, as he determined which of the applicants would be the best fit. He enjoyed greeting the small children each day when he arrived to check in on Lydia. Having his granddaughters and son nearby on the premises was a blessing. His pastoral duties had always dictated he have flexibility in his schedule, which also had meant he missed out on time spent with his children, grandchildren, and wife when important matters arose. Having his daughter in the secretary's office and his wife in the daycare tending to his granddaughters and his son made a huge difference in his life. He was able to steal more time with them in between calls and appointments and community crises. This new ministry also was a unique opportunity to reach more families in the community for Christ.

By the summer, the daycare had filled to capacity and had even been expanded to add room for more children and classes. A couple of the women in the church were hired to come in to help as the number of children grew. Saintly Mrs. Lincoln, whose grandchildren were all a little older than daycare age, wanted to come in and work a few days a week. She had a soft spot in her heart for children and they all loved her. The young mothers in the church all delighted in her handmade baby blankets and homemade treats on occasion. She was a perfect, grandmotherly addition to the staff. Another young lady, Amelia, had a couple of young girls of her own and was looking to add a little extra income to her household. Beacon Baptist Daycare had made it a policy not to charge staff members for the care of their own children. Being a ministry, the pay was not top-dollar, but the preacher wanted to set some specific incentives in place to help out the young mothers who may have a desire and gift to work in childcare. With these extra sets of hands, Lydia was able to structure meal times and learning center times with the children and the daycare really began to run smoothly. Many happy families called it home as their children learned, grew, and were taught about the love of Jesus.

With the success of the daycare came a new spark to an old dream. Rev. Englewilde had always had a burden to start a school. He had had the privilege of working for a couple of years at a Christian school when he was in Louisiana and he had loved it. He felt the burden to revisit the idea of founding a school at Beacon Baptist. He and Angelisa attended several training workshops to gain knowledge and insight into what would go into running a private church school. They knew it would mean hard work, but their facility had the space and they had the vision. After much prayer, they had the peace to continue. Work began immediately to convert old Sunday School rooms into school classrooms. Bathrooms were renovated and updated. Once again, Angelisa set out advertising the new school and its open enrollment. They knew they wanted to be somewhat selective when it came to choosing the right students. Only those families who were serious about receiving a Christian education were considered. There were some families who only sought to leave the public-school system or sought cheaper tuition than Christ Community School. If those were there reasons alone, they would probably not have enjoyed their experience at Beacon Academy.

Rev. Englewilde was not interested in being in competition with Christ Community School. He was still very much a part of the sports program there and was close personal friends with many of the staff members. He simply wanted to offer the community a school that would hold to the old paths, the old ways of teaching. He had a burden to instill godly principles and to teach respect and manners on a daily basis. He was one of the few preachers in Baldwin County that still held true to the King James Version and he felt burdened to keep its teaching alive in his community.

The excitement intensified as the first day of school approached. They had a total of seventeen kids enrolled. Rev. Englewilde's granddaughter Summer was one of the first to enroll in the kindergarten class, along with Amelia's oldest. Liam had been hired to teach Bible class and to help oversee the classrooms, in addition to his youth ministry duties. Several of the families within the church had enrolled their children and were excited to see how God would use this ministry to impact the community. One week before school was to start, the preacher fell extremely ill. Angelisa, extremely pregnant with her third daughter Daisy, was left to tend to the last-minute preparations for the school year as Lydia rushed the preacher to the emergency room. Unable to fully concentrate on the tasks at hand, she prayed for her father and hoped it would be nothing serious.

The physicians determined that Rev. Englewilde had precancerous polyps within the walls of his colon and surgery would be the only remedy. So, on the brink of launching the very first school year of Beacon Academy, Warren Englewilde underwent a major operation and had over twelve inches of his colon removed. Recovery would be painful and was recommended for longer than he was willing to sit still. Resting had never been Warren's strong suit. Neither had delegation, and he was forced to do both with literally no planning or preparation on his part. He had always been the one to rise up when emergencies presented themselves. He could not rise up this time. This time, it was his own medical emergency. Recovering from this would take longer than when the truck had fallen on him. Not since he was shot, roughly 25 years ago, had he been so incapacitated. It made him anxious not to be sitting in his church office, overseeing the church, daycare, and school. It would prove to be an extreme test of his patience and trust to allow Lydia and Angelisa to handle it all while he begrudgingly recovered at home from his operation. Somehow, they all managed to get through the trying ordeal and he was all set to return to his regular duties after only a few short, although seemingly long, weeks. The students greeted him upon his return with cards and signs and notes of encouragement. Slowly and carefully, he eased back into his busy schedule and routine, ever grateful for God's provision and for His mercy. He was so thankful to have had Lydia and Angelisa to help run things in his absence and to have Liam assisting with the church operations. While he had never been one to rely on the help of others, he was certainly blessed and thankful to have such a great staff that could maintain everything in his absence. God was surely blessing Warren Englewilde and his ministries in Baldwin County, Alabama.

Chapter 15

As the days passed, Rev. Englewilde slowly recovered from his surgery and found that his biggest struggle would actually be adhering to the doctor's suggested diet. Nothing delicious at all was on the list of allowed foods. Just bland, soft, flavorless options like baked chicken and buttered mashed potatoes. He thought for sure he would starve. No longer was he frequenting the Hardee's drive thru and scarfing down two of their delicious steak biscuits each morning. No longer was he allowed to wash down said biscuits with 32 ounces of Dr. Pepper. With such stringent dietary rules to follow and the loss of a large portion of his innards, he began to lose weight at a rapid pace. Not only did he feel like he was starving, he looked it as well.

Eventually, after several long months, he was able to slowly regain some tolerance for foods with a little flavor. By the time they wrapped up their third school year, he was back on the Dr Pepper and happily climbing back up on the scales. The school was rocking steady with an average of 18 students per year. The daycare had been consistently housing 12 full-time and 8 part-time enrollees. Using the daycare income to offset the cost of the school kept tuition low and affordable. This provided an opportunity for private education even to those families who had multiple children and may otherwise be unable to afford it. Things were running rather smoothly. They had been able to hire a new kindergarten teacher in the second year and her husband provided security on the property on nights and weekends in exchange for residence in the on-site apartment and employment in the school. They worked as a team and helped Liam grow the youth group and work the youth ministries. The one overcrowded van that Beacon Baptist started with had grown to a three-van fleet. One of those vans was used to bring in an average of 18 inmates from the local work release for weekly Sunday services. All aspects of ministry at Beacon Baptist Church were thriving and all throughout the Rosinton community and Baldwin County, people were hearing about the exciting work God was doing on that little piece of land.

Rev. Englewilde had always had a vision for his community and it was all coming to fruition before his eyes as he entered into the holiday season in 2009. Angelisa had just given birth to her fourth child, Isabelle, the summer prior and the school year had gotten underway with a record number of twenty-two students. The school was entering its fourth year and was set to have its first graduating class the following spring. As Fall settled in lower Alabama, the preacher began to look ahead to how he would like the very first graduation ceremonies to be planned. The staff agreed on a list of Scriptures for the student body to memorize throughout the school year and some of the students volunteered to do speeches, recitations, and skits. Everyone was working a little harder than usual to make sure everything would be planned well ahead of time and all the preparations would be done.

Spunky and Daniel Englewilde were now older and instrumental in their dad's ministry, even at 14 and 10 years old. They were leaders in the school, shining examples to their nieces Summer and Autumn, who were as close to them as sisters considering their ages of 8 and 6. Little Winston and Autumn were in kindergarten together and were the closest of all the Englewilde children and grandchildren. They were instant best friends from infancy, Autumn being only seven months older than her Uncle Winston.

Having recently had her fourth daughter, Angelisa quite possibly jumped back into her normal routine a bit early. At least, that was the general consensus when she came into the preacher's office one afternoon with ashen face and described an incident where she had passed out while driving with her four young daughters in the car with her. Sideswiping a mailbox with her passenger side mirror had jarred her back to consciousness just in time for her to regain control of the vehicle before any real damage was done. She had been only minutes from the church, so she swung in to tell her father of the fright she had just experienced. She wasn't sure what had happened or for how long she had been out of it. She just knew it had happened suddenly and she was afraid it may happen again.

A series of doctor's appointments would lead to some frightening conclusions and even further mysteries for Rev. Englewilde's daughter, Angelisa. She had continued to experience episodes of lost consciousness, to the point of no longer being able to drive. With her husband working increasing hours to cover the out-of-pocket expenses of multiplying doctor's visits, the preacher volunteered to be his daughter's transport to and from all appointments. It came to be that some weeks she had multiple appointments. Working became difficult and nearly impossible for her some days. It was evident why God had them begin planning the end of the school year at such an early date. Their attentions and efforts were to be spent trying to figure out why Angelisa was so sick, why she had suddenly begun losing consciousness at a rapid pace and with increasing frequency. At the age of 27 years old, she experienced an emergency hysterectomy brought on by medical complications. Hoping, this would result in relief of her symptoms, she reluctantly accepted that she would have no more children in the future. She held to the hope that the hysterectomy would be the answer to her medical puzzle while her preacher daddy held her hand throughout every appointment leading up to the surgery.

By the end of the school year, Angelisa was much worse and the hysterectomy had done nothing to stop her episodes of syncope, nor had it stopped her chronic migraines and nerve pain. Test after test was run as Rev. Englewilde drove his daughter from one clinic to another. When she was sent to Mayo Clinic for extensive testing, he was unable to leave his other obligations so Angelisa's mother took her while the preacher took over his daughter's duties at the school and in the office. It was a fast-paced and trying time for everyone. Angelisa's husband Easton stayed home from the trip to work and get Daisy and Isabella to daycare and Summer and Autumn to school each day. Their income had been cut drastically when Angelisa had fallen ill. He had taken an evening job delivering pizzas after he showered from his day job. Everyone was worn thin, drained both physically and emotionally.

Angelisa was finally diagnosed with two forms of dysautonomia - Neurocardiogenic Syncope and Postural Orthostatic Tachycardia Syndrome. Both had long names but can be boiled down to mean that when she changed positions, got overheated, was upset or excited or scared, her blood pressure would spike and then drop. Her body could not regulate the flight or fight mechanism, causing her to pass out when her condition was triggered. Teaching was far out of the question. They would need a reliable teacher to care for the children.

The kindergarten teacher and her husband had moved on to another job. Liam was preparing to be married. Rev. Englewilde was spread too thin. So, at the close of their fourth school year, Beacon Academy closed its doors.

Angelisa, young mother to four small girls, was rendered to be permanently disabled and would fight to gain an understanding of this sudden onset of illness. No one in her circle of peers had ever heard of it. Struggling with a mystery illness weighed heavy on her. Having her loving husband working hard each day was a comfort to her, knowing they were well taken care of. Having her father available when she needed a ride to the doctor's office was a blessing. They all worked together to create a new routine with differing responsibilities as they fought against the feelings of failure that crept in when they were reminded that there would no longer be a Beacon Academy.

The preacher continued to shepherd his flock while helping his daughter all he could. His parents were aging and needing more help on a weekly basis. His father had been struggling with pains and tremors. It was determined that he had Parkinson's disease and would need an increasing amount of help as he lost some of his fine motor skills. Most days were good, but there were days in which the struggle was greater as he fidgeted with the snaps on his western shirt. Warren took pride in helping his mother and father. They had always taken such good care of him. Even in adulthood, they had always been loving, supportive, Godly influences in his life. His mother Marie had always been his biggest cheerleader. She believed in her boys and loved them unconditionally while his father Forrest, a minister himself in his younger days, had led by Godly example and wisdom. Warren deeply respected both of his parents and vowed to care for them as much as they needed. He regularly drove the thirty some odd miles to drop in for a visit with them or to bring them lunch. As Angelisa's appointments slowed after she finally received a diagnosis, his parents' appointments increased. Slowly, his ministry became one of comfort and convalescence as he shifted gears to spend less time on the road with ball teams and prison ministries and more time ministering to his own family. His parents needed him. His daughter needed him. His wife and boys needed him. The preacher's heart was a servant's heart. He had given his life to the ministry of Christ, often going to visit the family members and loved ones of those who attended his church or lived within the community. He was finding that more often than not, those who were ill and suffering physically were his own loved ones. It made the ministry even more personal to him. He would give it his all, even when he felt he had nothing left to give.

Chapter 16

The phone fell to the floor. He sat there, numb with shock. His ears rang as a barrage of emotions flooded his body; first, shock, followed quickly by a mixture of bewilderment and disbelief. It felt as if he were trapped in a nightmare, watching the scene unfold but incapable of grasping the reality of what he had just been told over the phone. Nausea came in waves. He could not believe that, once again, he was being accused of a crime he did not commit. Not only was he accused, but he was to be charged. The investigator on the phone had been courteous in his request that Rev. Englewilde travel to his precinct in Mississippi and turn himself over to police custody. A warrant had been issued for his arrest and there was nothing left for him to do but to seek counsel and hope they could prove the 30-year-old allegations false. It was a classic "he said, she said" in which Rev. Englewilde faced some very serious accusations of an inappropriate relationship with a much younger female that held a maximum penalty of 30 years each in prison. There were a total of three charges and an active investigation was underway, in hopes to discover the truth of the matter.

The preacher gravely absorbed the gravity of this current situation. This time was so different from the last time he had faced false accusations over three decades prior. This time, he not only had a wife to worry about but he had a total of six children, half of whom were grown with families of their own. His throat constricted and his eyes were hot with unbidden tears as he thought of how this news would affect all those he loved. It had always been his natural inclination to feel some burden of responsibility when it came to the happiness of his family and to consider that this unforeseen devastation would wreak havoc on not only his family, but his entire congregation was almost too much to ponder.

The very accusations themselves took a toll on the preacher, but his family suffered greatly as well. They faced the possibility of losing their patriarch. His three grown children understood the full gravity of the situation and shared in the turmoil surrounding the uncertainty of the situation. His poor, sweet wife and three boys still at home had a multi-faceted dilemma as they faced the possibility of not only a physical separation from him but also a loss of income, should he be incarcerated and unable to provide for them. What would become of them, should everything go horribly wrong? Lydia would be so lonely without her beloved husband; he would be even more lonely without her. The faith of the preacher and his family was tested and Rev. Englewilde was wise enough to see this as a test and rallied to help his family to understand this. It was terribly difficult for him to maintain some semblance of bravery at times. The allegations were egregious and unfounded, but had to be investigated nonetheless. After he turned himself in for arrest, the men of the church had bail posted and a lawyer hired within minutes. The love and support of his congregation gave Rev. Englewilde and his family the courage and strength to hold together throughout the entire ordeal. Their faith had been tested in the past. Rev. Englewilde's impeccable memory could recollect with great detail all the times his faith had been tested and the lessons he had learned in each instance. This was not the first time his name and reputation had been dragged through the mud. He knew from experience that God would take care of him in every possible scenario that could play out. Should he be found guilty, he would preach in prison full time, a ministry he had enjoyed on a visitation basis but could hardly imagine as a full time resident of a penitentiary. He had to force himself somehow to prepare for that outcome while fervently praying that the truth would be found and that the nightmare would end. Every day was a battle – a battle within himself to remain calm and trust God.

Rev. Englewilde has many strengths, but he also has weaknesses. One of those weaknesses was and always will be the fact that he tends to worry over things. He trusts God absolutely, but he does have the tendency to imagine the worst of outcomes. While his faith in God was and remains strong, his faith in humanity had wavered over the years. He had seen the evil side of too many. He had seen the underhanded capabilities of the most unassuming of souls. Not only had he witnessed the worst in humanity, but he had also suffered as a result of it in more instances than he cared to recall. As this particular event unfolded in his life, he quickly began to question every relationship in his life in an attempt to make sense of why this was happening and why it was happening at that particular moment in time.

It didn't make sense to bring such allegations against someone from so many years ago. It didn't make sense to anyone. He wondered why this person would have waited so long if they had felt him guilty of such crimes for 30 years. He wasn't the only one wondering these things. The investigators also wanted to know why such allegations went untold for so long. A timeline of the three allegations made against Rev. Englewilde was provided by the plaintiff and it was found almost immediately that Rev. Englewilde and his family had not even resided in the state of Mississippi during the first year of the timeline. This being verified by many sources and it being evident that Rev. Englewilde had not even met the plaintiff until a year after the supposed first incident, there was now a light at the end of the tunnel. While the remaining investigation would not wrap up for another few months, the preacher and his family began to breathe a little easier.

Still, after this experience, a part of him always wondered about the motives and intentions of others. He realized then more than ever that the only surety is in Christ alone. Even the closest of friends can hold the most bitter of intentions.

It was eventually discovered that the allegations against Rev. Englewilde were the result of a desperate woman's attempt to gain pity in the eyes of a philandering husband. She mentioned the incidents in a marital counseling session with her husband in hopes that he would stay with her if he thought she was damaged. Her plan backfired when her husband insisted she press charges and testify to what she had alleged. This was his attempt to be the heroic husband she obviously wanted him to be. While the allegations were all eventually found to be false and the charges against Rev. Englewilde were dropped, the effect the ordeal had on him and his family remained permanently engrained in their minds as a reminder of what sinful humanity is capable of in moments of sheer desperation. One woman's desperate, distorted attempt to save her marriage had been the potential ruin of Rev. Englewilde, his wife, their three boys at home, their grown son, their daughters and their spouses, their grandchildren, as well as the entire church congregation at Beacon Baptist Church. Oh, what power the tongue possesses! One person's lie affected many lives. The worry, doubt, dread, and panic – all were caused by one person telling another person a story that they thought may produce some sympathy and pity for themselves without ever truly considering who all would stand to be hurt.

The Englewilde family had endured a rollercoaster of emotion throughout the entire ordeal, and had finally seen the charges dropped in time for Spunky to go off to college. When the preacher had adopted him and legally made him his own after marrying Lydia, they had given Spunky the chance to pick his name, considering he had only ever been known by his nickname. They decided that with a new last name, he could have an entirely new name altogether. While little Spunky's first choice was to be named Superman Walker Texas Ranger, Warren and Lydia had compromised with Forrest Walker Englewilde, Forrest being after his grandfather Forrest Englewilde. To the family, he would always just be known as Spunky. On the tail end of the whirlwind allegations and dismissal, Spunky was setting off to college a few hours away. He had surrendered to God's call on his life to preach the Gospel. Rev. Englewilde and Lydia could not have been prouder of their son than the day he told them he felt led to be a preacher of the Gospel of Jesus Christ. It was tough for Lydia to say goodbye to her boy as they dropped him off at his dorm. They had always had a very special bond and, for a while, it had just been the two of them against the world. Theirs was much like the bond Warren shared with his oldest daughter, Angelisa. Spunky understood his mother and held a soft place in his heart for her always. It was just as hard for him to watch her and his dad drive away as it was for them to leave him there.

They dropped Spunky off at college and by Christmas, he was officially introducing himself to the world as Forrest. After a couple of years, only those in his hometown knew who "Spunky" even was, but Forrest was *the MAN*. He dominated the soccer field his freshman year. He had always had a drive that was unlike any other. He had always been a fighter, always giving his all to any task. He had fought for his life as a preemie and he never quit trying to be everything he could be. He went on to dominate on the basketball court his freshman and sophomore years and won a state championship his senior year in college. He had grown to be the guy on campus that everyone looked up to, even though he only stood five foot six inches tall. The entire college campus, both students and staff alike, knew who Forrest Englewilde was by his impeccable character, reputation, and speaking ability. He had always been a storyteller as a child. His thirst for reading material outweighed all of his siblings' reading habits combined. Being an avid reader had developed within him a keen ability to draw and hold the attention of an audience, no matter how small or large the audience may be. Age didn't matter either. All were always captivated. His future was bright, even after such dark and recent circumstances surrounding his dad, the preacher. Forrest had learned, watching the only dad he had ever known all those years, that the power of God was, is, and always will be mightier than human comprehension. There were times in which he relied on the experiences and wisdom of his father to carry him through the rough times throughout his college life. As Spunky, he had gleaned much knowledge. As Forrest, he vowed to spread that knowledge to others.

Chapter 17

The preacher would ride that spiritual high of knowing his son Forrest had a blessed path laid before him as he pursued God's will for his life. With Daniel and Winston still in school and at home, Warren and Lydia felt the beginnings of what "empty nest syndrome" must feel. They had always had a lot of kids in the home. With six children come six sets of friends. As the number of children living under his roof dwindled down, the house started to feel quieter, older, more worn out and tired. It reflected the way Warren Englewilde felt most days. His dear father, and his son Forrest's namesake, had been battling illness. His father's struggle against Parkinson's Disease was a tremendously difficult thing for Warren, as well as his mother and two brothers, to witness. Rusty lived close by and helped whenever he could in between work assignments. Dan traveled a good bit for work and his free time was limited. In between business trips, he would stop in for a visit to brighten his mother's spirits. There's something about the baby son that always warms a mother's heart. Seeing the love of her life fight against such a cruel and unwavering illness was quite difficult for her. Warren spent two days each week taking his parents to appointments and helping them to keep the bills paid.

Forrest was born in 1932, back when real men still walked the earth – chivalrous, brave, and trustworthy. He had fought bravely in the Korean War, a time in his life of which he rarely spoke. After returning, he had married Marie, seven years his junior. She was still a senior in high school at the time and finished her classes at an alternative school. It was a time more innocent than those in which the world now lives. Married students were separated from the other students in an effort to protect the innocence of the high school populous. After Forrest and Marie had their three boys, Rusty, Warren, and Dan, he felt the call to preach. While maintaining his full-time job at the local mill, he began to preach on the weekends and, by the time he had reached his 80th birthday, he had earned quite a beloved reputation all along the Florida Panhandle. He was known for his even-tempered personality, much different from the personality of his middle son who followed in his pastoral footsteps. As his health failed him, the mercy and grace of God abounded in his life. With failing health came failing senses, the first of which to fade away was his hearing. No longer could Warren speak of the peaceful truths of Scripture with his father without shouting. Soon after, his memory began to slip. He often looked lost as he struggled to recollect who it was standing before him. And there were a lot of faces that visited him when he became homebound. A lifetime of ministering to others was repaid him in casseroles, pies, cakes, and warm hugs. One by one, his visitors were amazed at his one constant message. Even on the days when he could remember no one and seemed to talk of times long past and places long forgotten, he preached on this passage, his favorite passage, to each and every visitor:

John 14:1-6 (KJV)

Let not your heart be troubled: ye believe in God, believe also in me.
In my Father's house are many mansions: if it were not so, I would have told you. I go to prepare a place for you.

And if I go and prepare a place for you, I will come again, and receive you unto myself; that where I am, there ye may be also.

And whither I go ye know, and the way ye know.

Thomas saith unto him, Lord, we know not whither thou goest; and how can we know the way?

Jesus saith unto him, I am the way, the truth, and the life: no man cometh unto the Father, but by me.

His heart was not troubled, even in the end. He had preached the faithfulness and tenderness of Jesus Christ for decades. He had taught in love the Gospel of Christ. He was at peace and knew he was preparing to see his mansion, his place prepared by the very hands of God. He knew his time was nearing, even when he didn't know the time of day. Warren and his brothers gathered near their father in the days leading up to his passing. He grew weaker, yet his repeated message was as strong as ever. Rusty's two daughters, Layla and Melissa, took turns with their brother Preston visiting with their grandfather and holding their grandmother's hand. Warren's six children also drove over the state line to make more than their usual visits, as did Dan's daughter Beth. The grandchildren were saddened to know these were most likely to be their last days with the wizened patriarch of the Englewilde family.

Rusty, Warren, and Dan struggled to maintain their usually calm and even- keeled composures in times of distress. This was too close and personal for them all. They struggled, knowing that their father's days were nearing their end, but they also rejoiced in knowing his salvation was secure and he would soon be restored anew in the arms of Jesus their Savior. They had seen his suffering and had felt the hopelessness of not being able to relieve his suffering. They knew that his Heavenly body would far exceed even his best of days physically on this Earth. Saying goodbye was bittersweet, knowing his days of suffering on this Earth were soon to expire.

Forrest Englewilde passed away on July 5, 2014 in the wee hours of the morning. His passing was peaceful. His slumber was restful and he went quietly in his sleep, surrounded by people who loved him. Warren wept, instantly feeling a void that had been filled by his strong, Godly father. He knew he would need to be strong for his mother. It was his inherent character trait to be strong when others hurt. He was determined to be strong even when he hurt so deeply himself. He knew the promises of the Father. He knew that his dad's passing was only temporal and he would once be reunited with him in eternity. But he still ached and his soul was heavy as he sat holding his mother's frail hand. She had always had her devoted husband to take care of everything for her. She would now rely on her boys for that. He vowed right then and there to always be there when she called.

The funeral for the preacher's beloved father was unlike any other funeral ever witnessed by its attendants. It was a celebration of Forrest Englewilde's life. For hours, countless people filed through the viewing room and told stories of how he had touched their lives. There were tears of sorrow, but the tears of joy and gratitude far outweighed the sorrow felt. Hundreds of lives had been changed by the teaching, preaching and influence the old man had had on others throughout his life. He had lived what he had preached. He had never been quick to anger and had always helped others with his wise counsel and timely quoted scripture verses. Warren had always felt he lacked the particular gift his father had always possessed – to remain calm and reasonable in high-pressure situations. He strived to be more like his father as he himself aged. He and his brothers worked to make arrangements to care for their mother and to be sure she would not be lonely after the passing of her dear husband.

The passing of his father changed his life. He would not realize for some time to come, but his vision for his life was shifted somewhat, like a passing of the torch. He was now the patriarch of his own family line. He had a wife, six kids, and several grandkids – he often lost count at times – who looked to him for guidance. By that point, Angelisa and her husband had four daughters, Trinity Reese and her husband had one daughter, and Jacob had married Lilly Kindred and they had just had their first daughter. The number of grandchildren Warren and Lydia had seemed to change quite frequently. His children were happy and pursuing their own dreams. Angelisa had found a few treatment plans that had helped her to navigate her illness. She took advantage of her time on disability to both research her illness and return to school for a college degree. She had grown stir-crazy at home once her children were all in school and felt the best use of her time would be to further her education. Trinity Reese had married her high school sweetheart after graduating from LSU and they had worked as traveling medical professionals until the time finally came to start a family. While Trinity Reese had felt confident she would grant Warren his first grandson, she was somewhat perturbed to learn she would only add the fifth girl to the mix. Jacob, too, was blessed with a girl rather than a boy. Only time would tell if Rev. Englewilde should ever have a grandson at all. On the heels of his father's passing, Warren surveyed his life and saw that many precious loved ones relied on his counsel. He felt it all on his shoulders and felt resolved to care for each of them as their needs may arise.

Being ever-present for his family was not always the easiest feat while also pastoring a church. He had founded Beacon Baptist back in 1997. Almost 20 years later, he had seen the numbers in attendance go up and down and back up again. He had seen the birth of many ministries. Some of those ministries had run their course. Some had been quite successful, but those who worked them tirelessly had, indeed, grown tired and burnt out. Illness had struck some, his own daughter included, and limited their abilities to serve as they once did. Death had taken quite a few saints from his congregation and beloved community. He had seen a dozen men, both young and old, surrender to the call on their lives to preach. Some of those men thrived in the will of God. Some had lost sight of the importance of living for the Lord and had forgotten the peace they had experienced while thriving in the Will of God. With each and every individual's experiences and struggles, Rev. Englewilde took a piece of their burdens onto his own shoulders. There were days in which he felt weighted down with the cares, failures, disappointments, and struggles of all those for whom he felt solely and spiritually responsible. He internalized every problem for which he ever gave advice. When not very many were present for church services, he took it personally. He felt he had failed each time he pushed for a high attendance day and did not reach the mark. He felt he had failed when he saw his children make unwise choices, even those who were maneuvering adulthood. His burden for these people was great, so great that he let it weigh him down at times.

His crippled foot had deteriorated over the decades, always throbbing and causing him discomfort, thus adding to his daily struggles. The pain had been manageable for years, requiring the occasional surgery to remove scar tissue. Twice, he had gone under anesthesia to have it amputated, the nerve damage being irreparable and pain being unmanageable at times.

Once in his late twenties, he had been walking and felt a snap in the arch of his foot, once pieced and grafted together after the hunting accident he and Rusty had endured those many years ago. The bone graft had snapped in two and x-rays showed a break in the graft the size of the end of the preacher's little finger. He signed the papers to have his foot removed, resolved to make the most of the situation and focus on the possibility of less pain. He remembers quite often the feeling he felt when he came to in recovery. His head was clouded with the effects of the anesthesia wearing off. He thought in his mind that he could feel his toes wiggle. He paused, the sheet pulled up to his throat and clenched in both hands as fear gripped him, and he wiggled his toes again. He was sure that time that he definitely felt them wiggle under the sheet. He had heard of phantom pains in amputees and had hoped he would not be one of the ones to endure such potential agony. Slowly, he worked up the nerve to take a peek under the sheet to see what his footless ankle would look like. As he raised the sheet inch by inch to take a peek at the damage, he was amazed – and quite shocked – to discover the foot was still completely intact. Well, that is to say, as intact as it had been when he had gone under anesthesia earlier in the day. His doctor would later inform him that there was no medical explanation at all for him to give; nothing short of miraculous, in fact. The x-ray very clearly had shown a break. Another x-ray had been taken that morning prior to the operation. Both were precise and both showed the break. The doctor said when they opened up the foot, he wanted to see the break before beginning amputation; it had been sheerly on a whim and for the sake of curiosity. He wanted to take a look at it while it was viable and alive to see the extent of the damage. To his astonishment, he found that the graft was intact and whole, not broken or even cracked. There was no need to amputate the preacher's foot that day!

Now, with age, a little added weight, and years of wear and tear on his body, he wonders what life may have been like if they had been successful in amputating. The nerves in the foot had long been dead, causing him to walk on the ends of his toes, rather than on the pads of them. Years of compensating had led to a bad knee, bad hip, bad back, the list goes on. Some days had required a cane. Those days would come more and more frequently as time passed. He carried the burdens of the world on his shoulders, all on weakening knees and burning nerves. His faith helped him to endure, even when he felt he had no strength left. On one of his lowest of days, when he was feeling the especially heavy burdens associating with providing for his family, leading his flock, and caring for his mother, he was reminded of a truth while reading Mark 14: 3 *"And being in Bethany in the house of Simon the leper, as he sat at meat, there came a woman having an alabaster box of ointment of spikenard very precious; and she brake the box, and poured it on his head."* The Holy Spirit revealed to him in that moment the truth that to spend or be spent for the glory of Jesus is the greatest investment one can make in life! A box that is broken must pour out its contents. It is not wasted but exhausted. It has given its all, spent its last penny, breathed its last breath – all in an effort to benefit the Savior. If this was what his God should ask, this is the life he would live! It refreshed his soul in weary times and gave hope on his most burdened of days.

He kept this truth in mind and tried not to worry or show emotion when Angelisa and her family packed their belongings and moved to the northwest in search of a cooler climate. The heat had begun to take a toll on her physically and her doctors had recommended a change of climate to help combat her physical illness. Her husband had been blessed with a job offer and they had all been praying for peace concerning the decision. One by one, God had opened the doors to make their move a smooth transition. The Englewilde family had always been close, both geographically and metaphorically. To have Angelisa, her husband Easton, and their four girls move so far away would impact them in many ways. Special moments, both large and small, would no longer be shared in person. Warren was misty-eyed when he thought of all he and Angelisa had gone through throughout her lifetime. She had grown from his little girl, to his co-laborer in Christ at Beacon Baptist, to his friend. There would never be another secretary quite like her, at least not in his eyes. He rejoiced with her as she embarked on her cross-country journey to relocate, even as his daddy heart grieved to know she was leaving.

The year after Angelisa relocated, Trinity Reese and her husband took jobs at a local practice. This allowed them the opportunity to raise their daughter Kay Lynn in their home town near her grandparents. They had traveled for work in their early twenties and were ready to settle down near family in their thirties. With Daniel preparing to go to Bible College after surrendering to youth ministry, the Englewilde house was often too quiet for comfort. Angelisa's girls all lived too far away for frequent visits. Jacob's girls were two little yet to be left with grandparents for very long, and Kay Lynn was busy with her own extracurricular activities after preschool at Christ Community School. Winston kept himself busy his freshmen year with every sport he could possibly play. It would be lonely being the last kid at home. He did enjoy having a room to himself. Rev. Englewilde had been able to build his family a new house right after Spunky left for college. Winston loved that the house had been built as most of the kids were leaving home. It had given him an advantage over the rest of them. He had never been forced to share a room. He had, in fact, chosen to but that was altogether different in his eyes. He had a mischievous grin on his face that always seemed to let on that he knew he was a bit spoiled but just didn't care who else noticed. He also had a heart of gold and everyone noticed that regardless.

The preacher's life was altogether different than it ever had been before. His mother struggled more and more each day with illness. She was frail at times. But other days, she rallied and was perky and ready to shop. He began to more eagerly look forward to his days with her. She would make a list of errands she needed to run. Sometimes, she'd need to go to the bank. Sometimes it was the grocery store. Other days it was the pharmacy. Almost always, she would want to eat at the buffet. When she grew sicker, those days together were more often spent going to pulmonologists and cardiologists. On those days, she didn't eat as much and barely touched her cobbler. Those days made Warren sad. He would go home and pray for his sweet mother. He would text his kids to do the same. Often, he shared with his congregation how his mother was doing. Many of them had grown to love her as they got to know her better, as people tended to do. Marie was a saint with the voice of an angel. She had always used her singing ability to bless others. She had always loved to visit nursing homes and bless those sweet souls encumbered by illness with a song and a prayer. When she became her sickest and was herself placed in a rehab facility until she was strong enough to return home, visitors from all over the Florida panhandle came to sing and to pray with her. As much as she had always loved to encourage others, that encouragement was repaid tenfold when she had needed it the most. Whether it was to transport her to the corner store or to the doctor's office across town, Warren realized his newest calling on his life was to be the support for his mother that she had always been to him and to others.

Now that he was years older and, arguably, much wiser, he found himself reflecting upon his life with different eyes than he had when his ministry had first begun. He had started preaching at 15 years old. The young man he had been was a dreamer and often acted first and thought later. As a man with experience in pain, disappointment, victory, and defeat, he saw things with less grandeur than he had in his days of youth. He missed the wise counsel of his father, who had always been slow to act and methodical in his reasoning. He cherished the company of his dear mother. His relationship with his children had almost completely shifted now that they were all growing or already grown. His need to guide their choices had lessened as they had developed the skills to somewhat manage adulthood themselves. Angelisa, Trinity Reese, and Jacob all had spouses and families of their own. Forrest and Daniel were both away at Bible College. And Winston was well into high school. The preacher found that he had more free time to do the little things he once found difficult to accomplish. He and Lydia found time in those days to sneak away for lunch at the Waffle House or the Shrimp Basket. The next stage in his ministry and in his life would be a very different one, although he was yet unaware of the changes that lie ahead of him.

Chapter 18

Any sense he had made of his life thus far came crashing in on him the day he received the panicked call from his dear wife Lydia. The fear and uncertainty in her usually calm voice were apparent the moment he had answered the phone. She was calling from work. She had been rocking a baby in the daycare and had suddenly felt very weak. After passing the child off to her co-worker, she had stood up from the chair, only to have her legs fail to hold her up. She crumpled to the floor unable to move them for several moments. Concerned, her co-workers insisted she call him to get her from work early. He was at a loss for words, a new sensation for the preacher. Lydia was his rock. She balanced him out. She was his sounding board on his bad days, his encourager when he felt his lowest, and his voice of reason when his emotions got the best of him. She had been the one beautiful constant in a life filled with upsets and chaos. To know she was suffering and scared broke his heart. But he felt he must remain strong for her, especially for her.

That had been the first of many such episodes. She lost the sensation in her arms at times. They grew heavy and weak, unable to be moved by sheer will. She was eventually forced to quit her job. It scared her to know she could hurt herself or even a child, never knowing when the muscles and nerves in her legs and arms would go limp and refuse to work for her. One doctor visit led to another, then another. Days morphed into weeks and weeks into months as the preacher transported his ever-suffering bride from one test to another in hopes of finding answers. They both grew weary, meeting with one new doctor, then another, always searching for answers and never getting any at all. Just more tests and more co-pays. With her income gone and mounting medical debt, they were struggling to stay afloat financially. Beacon Baptist had not given Rev. Englewilde a pay increase in quite a few years, which had never really bothered the preacher, but he was struggling and had no idea how to bring it up with the men without sounding greedy. He had never been in the ministry for the money. That was painfully evident by his ability to stretch his dollars out between paychecks and lack of savings. He felt that his time spent with his wife in search of answers was somehow detracting from his ability to minister; therefore, he would not mention a pay raise to anyone. He would simply do his best to be a good steward of what God had given him.

As he and Lydia constantly jumped through all the hoops the medical professionals could hurl at them, he struggled to maintain his pastoral duties as well. He also continued to care for his mother. He was very quickly being stretched too thin and his own health began to reflect that. He quickly lost a lot of weight. He was eating most of his meals on the go and rarely stopped to rest or take a breath. Lydia had lost the ability to drive. Some days, he drove to take his mother to appointments in the morning only to return across the Alabama state line to assist his wife with her own appointments. Often times, Lydia could not maneuver through the house to cook or do household chores. She had quickly been reduced to using a walker to get around. How it broke his heart to see his young wife suffering and unable to get around like she so recently had been able to do!

The faithfulness of God sustained them. As they fought to get Lydia on disability without an actual medical diagnosis, hope was deferred time and time again. At long last, they were forced to hire a disability lawyer. All that meant was there would be someone who understood the laws who would fight on her behalf. He would also take a giant portion of her disability payment, should it ever be granted. Naturally, the lawyer too took his time; the longer the battle, the bigger the check. The entire process was lengthy and exhausting. Lydia was left to request all of the records for every appointment, tests, and procedure. None of those had helped her gain any answers at all, but she was instructed to prove she was trying, at least, to find a diagnosis.

Pastoring and caring for his wife and mother were often a strain on his physical body. Warren awoke tired every morning. He was often in his office before 7 a.m. trying to get a jump start on the day before the phone began to ring with questions, concerns, requests for prayer, etc. His breakfasts were often steak biscuits and Dr Pepper from Hardee's as he left Loxley and headed to see his mother over the state line in Escambia County. A typical visit at her house would result in the paying of her bills, the checking of her mail, and the running of her errands and then he was back in Loxley again for lunch with his sweet wife. His afternoons were spent visiting the sick and absentees from church and getting Winston from school or practice. His evenings were spent with his wife when he wasn't preaching a service in a prison somewhere. That ministry was still thriving and God was doing a mighty work behind bars using Rev. Englewilde in a powerful way. He was also fitting in his own household errands wherever and whenever he could. With Lydia unable to drive and cook, these chores fell to him as well. From the very moment that he had met her, she had impacted his life in the most positive of ways and he did not mind for one second when he was taking care of her. Often, his frustration was misinterpreted to be aimed at her but that was never his intention. He was frustrated that she should have to suffer and struggle so much on a daily basis. At any point he would willingly take it all on himself if he could. She was in his prayers constantly. As they continued to seek the advice of myriad medical professionals and physicians, they both grew more and more discouraged with each and every dead-end they encountered. Slowly, Lydia came to rely on him more and more.

It was not only the nerves in her arms and legs any longer. She began to have difficulty swallowing, causing her to have issues eating. At times, her face was completely numb, as was her throat. She began to have painful spasms in her temples. She would sit for hours on some days and cry from the pain and uncertainty of her worsening situation. Even as her health continued to decline, doctors were unable to pinpoint the problem. This only led to heightened levels of fear and dread as she and Warren struggle to make sense of their endless medical nightmare. Not even the doctors at the Mayo Clinic could find a definitive answer, despite the doctors all being renowned in their fields. The prayers of the people at Beacon Baptist, as well as those in neighboring churches and across the country, all focused on Lydia Englewilde. While the doctors were unable to give her any answers, it encouraged her spirit to know that so many saints had her name on their lips when they spoke to the Almighty Father.

After a couple years of chasing after the hope of finding answers, Lydia began to struggle even when she was sleeping. A sleep study showed that her brain was forgetting to tell her lungs to breathe as she slept each night. The study showed that she would stop breathing about thirty times each night. The doctor concluded in his findings that the problem with her breathing was absolutely related to her other problems. He just didn't know what exactly the problem was yet. At the news of hearing all of this, Lydia felt that her biggest fear – the hereditary acquisition of the same illness that had gripped her mother – was coming to fruition. While no one could definitively tell her what she feared was true, she had always known it to be a possibility. She had known it since her own mother had fallen ill when Lydia was just a young girl. She had known the possibility for all those years she had spent nursing her mother in a hospital bed in her childhood living room. She had known it and had prayed against it. But she also knew that God had a plan, even in illness. Her mother had been a saintly woman herself. She had influenced so many throughout her years of sickness and suffering. It had been incredibly difficult for Lydia to have her mother on life support for the better part of her life. She had never wanted that for her own children. While she had loved her own mother so desperately and had spent a great deal of her early adult years helping her sister care for her, she had always hoped that her own health would be better and not cause her to be a strain on her own children. This sentiment was not shared by her own boys. They did not care what it took, they wanted their mother taken care of and they knew their father was doing a good job. They also knew he too was aging and they were willing to help in any way they could.

They did not mind giving her the care she needed, as she had done for them as they were growing up.

Determined not to one day rely on machines and medicines for the most basic of senses, Lydia made the choice to deny any future measures that would require life support. She knew what may lie ahead, even if her children could not grasp it all. Warren also knew. He had helped with Lydia's mother when they had first been married. He had seen what all it had entailed to care for someone in such a state at home. He had seen firsthand the emotional and physical toll it could take, let alone the financial toll. He was willing to give his all and then some to care for his wife. She knew that. She knew her boys and her stepchildren loved her and would also do whatever it took. She knew because she had felt the same way about her own mother. So, she took the decision off of their shoulders. She would not allow them the opportunity to put everything on hold indefinitely on her account. She signed the proper forms and put everything in place to refuse any measure of life support, should she ever need it.

Chapter 19

With Lydia's mind made up, the course upon which his life would follow became resoundingly clear. She was the love of his life. He had known it from the first moment he had laid eyes on her. She had henceforth been his balancer in life. On his discouraged days, she had offered encouragement. On the days he felt his sermons fell flat on deaf ears, she had offered her loving support. On his days of victory, she cheered him. When he had found himself most tired, she was the rest that his heavy heart needed. She was his comfort. They had gone through pain and loss together. They had grown stronger together. Their faith had become deeply rooted in God as they strove to serve Him as one. God had granted him his soulmate in that petite woman and he vowed in his heart to care for her, whatever the cost. He desperately wanted to show her what she meant to him. He knew with absolute certainty what needed to be done.

With Forrest and Daniel both finished with Bible College and seeking employment in the ministry, the pieces were falling together and Warren could see God's plan for his life, his sons' lives, and the future of the ministries at Beacon Baptist Church. Baldwin County had given him so much more than ministry opportunities. It had given him a home, a loving wife, and three children he had never dreamed he would have. It had offered him friendships and fellowship with some pretty incredible believers. Baldwin County, Alabama had grown in his heart and it would forever have a place there. After two and a half decades, he felt the peace of God assuring him that the time had come to make changes.

First, he met with Vern. Vern had been his right-hand man since almost the first day he had come to Baldwin County. From maintenance around the church to running sound equipment to engine repairs on the church vans and the pastor's personal vehicles, Vern did it all. He was a jack of all trades and had a heart of gold. He did not care to be up front and in the spotlight, so to speak, but he was always faithful to do whatever was needed around the church. He kept the grass cut during the summer. He always brought the ice to church functions and events. He worked tirelessly to be sure the air conditioners were always in working order around the church property. He kept things going behind the scenes and took care of the things people only seem to notice when they are broken. He had grown to be a true and trusted friend to Warren Englewilde and the preacher relied on his calm demeanor as a sounding board whenever there was church business to discuss. He knew that Vern would be a good person to start the conversation with about the future prospects of Beacon Baptist Church. The preacher knew the changes that needed to be made and he wanted to make sure that the transitions within the church would go smoothly and effortlessly.

His next meeting was between him and his two preacher sons. Forrest and Daniel had both received degrees in ministry and were surrendered to God's call on their life. They had sought counsel and prayed concerning what God would have them do in the area of ministry. They had both returned to Baldwin County after college to be closer to their mother after she had fallen ill. Forrest had taken a job at Christ Community School as a teacher and coach. Already, he was following in his father's footsteps. He had an exciting way of teaching and preaching that really captivated the attention of his listeners. Daniel had taken a job at a local business in town. He did side jobs with Jacob and had quite a knack for carpentry and wood-working. The brothers had always been too similar in personality to work for very long together, but they were both extremely talented in the field so Daniel used his connection to his big brother to gain quite an impressive job in town. He had built for himself a reputation of being a hard worker, a trait that all the Englewilde children seemed to share. The two brothers were willing and open to the leadership of the Holy Spirit. When Rev. Englewilde sat down with the young men to discuss the potential of one of them, if not both, coming to take staff positions at the church, he was amazed and a bit surprised to find they had already been talking about that possibility between themselves. They knew they had both surrendered. They knew that, despite being offered many other offers across the country, they wanted to be in Baldwin County. They knew the strain that the past few years had taken on their dad and they knew how much their mother needed him. They knew and were willing to pray and seek God's will concerning their part in all of it.

After much counsel and prayer, Rev. Englewilde finally had peace. He knew that his days at Beacon Baptist Church were drawing to an end. Not only did he know it, but he had peace about it. It was an inexplicable peace that calmed his soul and steadied his mind. He had never dreamed that the day of his retirement would ever come. He had always imagined he be in the pulpit until the Lord saw fit to take him home to eternity in Heaven.

The call to preach had been placed on his life at such a young age. At first, he had fought that call as a young 14-year-old boy. He fought it and had kept it hidden internally as a secret between him and God. God had not given up. God had gotten ahold of his heart and changed his life and he had been preaching since he was fifteen. He had never looked back. He had never wavered. He had always preached with all the energy and gumption the Lord could bestow upon him. The power he had always felt when he was preaching the

Gospel was immeasurable. He never felt crippled or tired or discouraged when he was standing before sinners, and believers alike, expressing the love and truths of the Bible. He had always enjoyed helping to disciple young Christians and watching their faith grow as a result. He had never wanted to even think about doing anything else with his life. During those years when his preaching was inhibited by the stigma and judgment of fellow saints, he had felt his lowest and had lacked purpose. He had never wanted to feel that way again.

But this time he knew was different. This was God-inspired. He felt it. His sweet Lydia needed his ministering heart more than any other. She was hurting. She was struggling. She was growing more and more discouraged with each and every test, procedure, and appointment. He wanted more than anything to wipe away her tears for good and to take all her pain and hurt upon himself. He knew that only Christ could do such miraculous works. Still, he prayed. He hoped for a miracle in his wife's life. He marveled at how she maintained an attitude of gratitude throughout all of her trials. No matter what she was going through or how badly she was hurting, she still had that same sweet temperament and calming presence she had always had. In her years of physical adversity, she had grown to be one of the strongest prayer warriors he had ever known. Her tender heart was burdened for those she knew who were also struggling with their own problems. She was unable to do much, but she had never lost her ability to reach the throne of God with her prayers. If the righteousness of saints exalts a nation, then Lydia was certainly doing her part in the heart of Baldwin County.

As the Lord was guiding the preacher and preparing his heart for what was to come, He was always guiding and preparing Forrest and Daniel as well. Daniel had always enjoyed teaching and preaching to younger listeners. As a teenager himself, he had helped with many youth and children's ministries at Beacon Baptist. He had gone to Bible College to pursue a degree in youth ministries and had excelled in his classes. He had returned with a renewed vision for the young people of Baldwin County. The Rosinton community was much larger than it had been when Rev. Englewilde had first moved into the community. So many growing families had moved into the well-sought-after area and the church had also experienced growth in the process. Forrest had a good rapport on the campus of Christ Community School and was instrumental in reaching many young people for Christ through his jobs there. The two brothers were just as well-known in the area as their dad and had developed the reputation to be men of integrity and faith. As they worked within the community, they prayed for guidance and clarity as they looked ahead to what God may have them to do.

They, too, received the peace from God that they sought and their minds and hearts were set to do what they were called to do.

Beacon Baptist Church was gearing up to celebrate its 25th anniversary. Arrangements were made to fly Angelisa and her family in to provide special music for the day. The ladies of the church all rallied to plan one of their delicious southern-style buffets, complete with crispy fried chicken, homemade mashed potatoes and gravy, and sweet corn from their gardens. The men of the church all gathered on the day before the event to clean the gutters, weed the flower beds, and touch up the paint in the hallways. The sanctuary was decorated with photos and memories of the 25 years they had all shared. The parking lot was swept and the glass doors wiped clean of handprints. Every little detail was planned out. It was to be a family-style gathering with people from all over the community coming together to celebrate the momentous anniversary of the founding of Beacon Baptist Church. A secret offering was collected by the faithful members of the congregation to be sure to bless their dearly loved Pastor Englewilde and his sweet saint of a wife Lydia. Everything was in order.

Rev. Englewilde sat in his office in the early Sunday morning hours, contemplating the day and the celebration to come. His heart was somewhat heavy with the weight of knowing what all the day would entail. While he had peace in his soul, there was always a part of him that feared uncertainty. He would announce during the service that he would be retiring to care for his wife. He would announce that Forrest would be filling his place in the pulpit as an interim pastor and he would announce that Daniel would be his assistant pastor. Only a handful of people knew that these announcements would be made at the close of the morning's service. He wanted with all his heart for his congregation to be open to the news and to be receptive to what the Lord had already revealed to him and his sons concerning the leadership of Beacon Baptist. He prayed fervently for the movement of the Holy Spirit throughout the service and congregants that day. He had prayed throughout the night previous and he had prayed for weeks prior to that. As he stood from his desk and surveyed his office, he was flooded with memories.

There were the memories of kneeling in prayer beside those hurting and in need of spiritual comfort. There were memories of those who had sought his counsel in their marriages. There were memories of he and Angelisa crying and praying when she had fallen ill herself and had so many questions that lacked answers from the medical community. There were happy memories of his grandchildren running in after Sunday School and asking him for peppermints. He had memories of late-night prayer sessions. All these memories and more flooded him as he took it all in. Emotions of all sorts hit him and tears pricked the corners of his eyes as he reflected back on all the sweet and bittersweet memories that Baldwin County had given him. He loved the people dearly and had only always wanted one thing: for the grace and mercy of God the Father to be known throughout the community because of his time spent at Beacon Baptist Church. He wiped his tears and checked his hair one last time as he readied himself. Resolved, he stepped out into the hall and greeted those who anxiously anticipated the excitement of the day.

Epilogue

As he sits and reflects on all that has transpired over the course of his ministry, he sees things much clearer now than he did as a fresh young preacher boy. He sees the regret. He sees the hurt. He sees the thousands of tiny alterations he could have made along his journey. But he also sees the joy and pride of a life well-lived and a job well done. Not for one second has he ever regretted giving his life to Christ. Not for one second has he ever second-guessed the calling God placed upon his life all those years ago as a young teenager. Sure, life has not always dealt him an easy lot, but it has brought him closer to his Heavenly Father and has taught him the value of true faith. It has taught him loss and pain and longsuffering. He has learned over the course of time of the fallacy of man. He has experienced the pure grace of God in circumstances that seemed so bleak and trying. Within every fiery trial, there is a lesson of grace and mercy. Along each weary mile, there is peace and assurance of the love and faithfulness of his Heavenly Father. In times of sorrow, sadness, and loss, his faith has sustained him through and granted him the ability to emerge, time and time again, wearing a happy smile. Life here on out will be different. He is wiser now; kinder in some ways. His experiences have softened him. He will rest now in the precious assurance of the Gospel, knowing the Lord's will is being done and he will trust God to lead him as he embarks upon perhaps his scariest journey yet: retirement.

Made in the USA
San Bernardino, CA
09 April 2020